THE WEEKEND

Peter Cameron is the author of the novel *Leap Year* and the short-story collections *One Way or Another* and *Far-Flung*. His fiction has appeared in *The New Yorker*, *Rolling Stone* and *The Paris Review*. He lives in New York City and works for the Lambda Legal Defence and Education Fund.

THE WEEKEND

Peter Cameron

FOURTH ESTATE • *London*

First published in Great Britain in 1996 by
Fourth Estate Limited
6 Salem Road
London
W2 4BU

Copyright © 1994 by Peter Cameron

The right of Peter Cameron to be identified as the author of
this work has been asserted by him in accordance with the
Copyright, Designs and Patents Act 1988

A catalogue record for this book is available from the
British Library

ISBN 1–85702–449–4

1 3 5 7 9 8 6 4 2

Printed in Great Britain by
Clays Ltd, St Ives plc

FOR NORBERTO

Catherine thought, perhaps if we travel together, I shall get to know them at last, for so far I have been all wrong, and they have turned out different to what I thought. How is one to know what people are like? . . . Perhaps one can never know; perhaps people are uncapturable, and slip away like water from one's hand, changing all the time.

—ROSE MACAULAY
Staying with Relations

Violence gathers in a small place: a room, a bed, a glove.

—JAMES SCHUYLER
"The Infant Jesus of Prague"

THE WEEKEND

For a few minutes after the sun rose the world was quiet and still and everything human seemed far away, as if the tide had gone out. Marian would leave John and Roland sleeping in the house and walk down the damp green lawn toward the river, barefoot, in her nightgown.

She could not say that the river was loveliest in the morning because on those still evenings when it turned purple, almost seemed to stop flowing, and lay like a bruise at the end of the lawn, it could make her cry. But in the morning there was nothing emotional about it. It was deep and cold and purposeful, clearer and curative.

She'd walk upstream a ways to a secluded spot where some trees had fallen, creating a still pool with a sandy bottom. She waded for a moment, and then slipped into the water and swam quietly, almost surreptitiously, hardly moving the water, allowing it to move her. Then she lay for a while on the dock, feeling the chill of the river passing beneath her and the not-quite-warmth of the early sun rising above, and herself, her body, in between, solid and clean, alive.

At some point she would sense that John or Roland had awoken—it was just a feeling that the house was no longer asleep. She'd stand and begin to walk up toward it. She felt a happiness rise in her as she mounted the lawn. Her house and her garden and the river—they gave her such pleasure; it was all so beautiful, every stone and window and leaf.

Her delight was so keen it almost hurt.

2

Robert was late and for a few minutes Lyle feared that he had changed his mind and wasn't coming. This made absolute sense to Lyle: it had been absurd to think, he thought, that Robert would come. In fact, I am relieved, he managed to convince himself. But then he caught sight of Robert hurrying across the thronged plaza of Grand Central, a glimpse before he disappeared, only to reappear closer, and every time Robert reappeared, closer and larger, Lyle's doubt diminished, until Robert was there, standing beside him, grinning and panting, and Lyle's doubt was gone.

The train was crowded, and they were unable to get adjoining seats. The crowd bothered Lyle, who liked to think that when he was escaping from the city he was doing it alone; to be accompanied by a trainload of brightly dressed people clutching shopping bags stuffed with wine and baguettes spoiled his pleasure. From where he sat on the aisle, next to a woman wearing a delft-print sundress, he could see the back of Robert's head, three rows forward. Lyle was a little jealous because Robert was sitting next to a handsome young man wearing hiking boots and shorts. They would talk and flirt and fall in love, Lyle feared, but as far as he could tell, they had not yet spoken a word to one another.

Lyle had brought the newspaper with him, but he felt too distracted to read it. He looked past the delft woman—she was reading *Elle*—out the window at the river, flowing in the opposite direction of the train. It wasn't at all how he had pictured the ride. He had foolishly thought that the train would be empty, just Robert and him sitting next to—or opposite perhaps, facing—one another, talking quietly as the river flowed past and the train sped forward. Lyle had wanted to use the journey to prepare Robert, to tell him about his friends, John and Marian, at whose house they were spending the weekend. And to tell Robert a little about Tony, too, for there was no way to talk about John and Marian and not talk about Tony. It was all connected. Or it had all been connected.

Two men sitting opposite Lyle got off at Croton. He threw his bags over onto the empty seats and walked up the aisle to fetch Robert. As he approached he saw that Robert was talking animatedly to the hiker, and he was struck again by Robert's youth and beauty. Does he look like that when he talks to me? Lyle wondered. He lost his nerve, and instead of asking Robert to join him on the seats he had staked, he said, "I'm going to the café car. Can I get anything for anyone? A coffee?"

"I'd like coffee," said Robert.

"What about you?" Lyle asked the hiker, as if they were all friends. "Can I get you a coffee?"

"No thanks," the man said.

Lyle squeezed Robert's arm, briefly, possessively, and

then continued up the aisle. The ripe, warm feeling of Robert's flesh lingered, as if it were a fruit Lyle still palmed. When he returned a few minutes later, Robert was reading a magazine, and the hiker was looking out the window.

"There are two seats free back there," Lyle said. "Come sit with me."

"O.K.," said Robert. He stood up and gathered his bags. "Take care," he said to the hiker, who smiled and nodded.

The delft woman lowered her magazine and watched them settle into their new seats. People never want to be sat next to, Lyle thought, yet they are always offended when you desert them.

Lyle handed Robert a coffee from the cardboard raft, which also contained a Danish pastry smothered in plastic wrap. "I got that for you," said Lyle. "I didn't know if you'd had breakfast."

"Yes," said Robert, "but thanks."

"What were you talking about?" asked Lyle.

"What?"

"With the hiker? The guy you were sitting next to."

"Oh. He asked me where I get my hair cut. And then he told me he was going hiking at Monadnock."

"Why did he ask you where you get your hair cut?"

"I don't know. I guess he liked it. He needed a haircut. His girlfriend used to cut his but they broke up."

"Where do you get your hair cut?"

"Nowhere particular. Just from different people. A woman at Skowhegan gave me this one." Robert shook his head a little to show it off. He had beautiful hair: long and very black, cut with an almost excruciating bluntness. It seemed to be the one feature of his beauty about which he was aware, and perhaps a little vain. Robert sipped his coffee and then said, "How much longer?"

"Till we get there? A while yet. At least an hour," said Lyle.

"I'm nervous," said Robert.

"Why?" asked Lyle.

"I don't know. I'm always nervous about meeting new people. Tell me about them."

A delicious sort of shiver ran through Lyle. What I wanted to happen is happening, he thought. For a moment he felt the rest of his life unfurling like that, ordained and golden, as effortless as falling, but the sense of falling reawakened the terror with which he normally regarded the future.

Robert was unswaddling the Danish. Lyle waited until he had taken a bite of it. "John and Marian are the nicest people I know," he began. "They are my best friends. Marian, especially."

"How long have you known them?"

"John and I were roommates at college. And Marian I met in graduate school. So a very long time. About twenty years."

"Did you introduce them to each other?"

"Yes," said Lyle. "I suppose I did. In a roundabout way."

"How romantic," said Robert. "Do you want a bite?" He offered the Danish.

"O.K.," said Lyle. His appetite was not for the pastry; it was for the act of sharing it. He leaned forward and took a bite. "It's awful," he said.

"Yes," said Robert. He put the pastry down. "What do they do?"

"What do you mean?"

"I mean John and Maryanne. Do they have jobs?"

"It's Marian," said Lyle. "M,A,R,I,A,N. Marian."

"Oh," said Robert.

"It's just that she hates it when people call her Maryanne," said Lyle.

"I'll make sure to call her Marian," said Robert. "What do they do?"

"Well, nothing, really. John worked for American Express, but he quit last year. And Marian used to restore paintings but she hasn't worked much recently, since they moved upstate. Neither of them has to work. John is very wealthy. Both of his parents were extremely rich."

"So what do they do all day?"

"They do—things. John has a huge garden, and Marian . . . Well, they live a life of leisure, to be perfectly honest, but they do it very well. You'll see. They're not aimless. And of course there's Roland, now, to look after."

"Roland is a child?"

"Yes," said Lyle. "What else would he be?"

"I don't know," said Robert. "A pony, or a spiritual advisor."

Lyle laughed, but a little disapprovingly, for one did not joke about Roland. "No," he said. "Roland is a child. He's my godson."

"How old is he?"

"He was born last summer." Just after Tony died, Lyle thought. Tony's death and Roland's almost simultaneous birth unnerved him a little. It linked them in a way that he knew was nonsensical but nonetheless made him feel, if he allowed himself, uncomfortable. "Roland's just about a year. I've brought him some paints."

"Do you see them often?"

Lyle paused a moment. "I used to come up every week-end, almost, with Tony. But I haven't been up at all this summer. This is the first time."

"Why?" asked Robert.

"Oh, I've been busy," said Lyle. "I was at Skowhegan, for instance."

"That was only for two days."

"Yes," said Lyle. "But I haven't really felt like it this summer. I've been content to stay in the city. Actually, you were the catalyst. I was thinking of not going."

"Why not?"

"Oh, inertia, mostly. And I didn't think I would have much fun going by myself. Or be much fun, for that matter."

"And what difference do I make?"

Lyle looked at Robert. His face was set, on the brink of something, waiting.

"You've made a big difference," said Lyle. He tried to choose his words carefully. He wanted to be accurate, and honest. "Ever since I met you I've felt much less dreary. I know I was depressed and I suppose I still am, but the difference is that—well, now I see an end to it. Or a respite, at least. It's different from before. It frightens me, a little, actually."

"Why?" asked Robert.

"Because . . ." Lyle paused. "My life—when you've been alone in your life in the way I've been alone, you may be sad, and you may be lonely, but you have control of your life, because you have complete possession of it. And then when you meet someone—when something like this happens—you feel, one feels—*I* feel—I feel that control vanishing. And that frightens me."

"You could change your mind," said Robert. He was looking out the window.

"About what?" asked Lyle.

"About this, our coming here, together." He turned to face Lyle. "I mean, I'd understand if you did. I could just take a train back to the city."

"Don't be ridiculous," said Lyle. "Why would I change my mind?"

"I don't know," said Robert. "I just wanted to let you know that if you did, it would be O.K."

"No, it wouldn't," said Lyle.

"Do Marian and John know I'm coming?"

"Of course they know you're coming."

"And they don't think it's strange?"

"Of course not," Lyle said. "They're eager to see me, and they seemed very happy that I was bringing someone along. It means they have to entertain me less. It will be your job, you see, to keep me entertained." Lyle picked up Robert's hand, and examined it as an excuse for holding it. "You have very elegant fingers," he said. "Do you play the piano?"

"No," said Robert.

"Well, you have the fingers of a pianist," said Lyle. He kissed them.

Robert bit his lip to stop his smile, and turned his face a little, toward the window, but Lyle could see the skin on his cheek tremble and flush. He turned to Lyle and said, "And what about Tony? Did they like Tony?"

"Of course they did," said Lyle. He heard the terseness in his voice, and added, "John and Tony were half brothers."

Robert turned away from the window. "Half brothers?" he asked. "What do you mean?"

"They had the same mother. John's parents divorced, and John's mother moved to Italy. Tony was born there. It's less complicated than it sounds. Or perhaps it's not."

"How did you meet him?"

"Tony? I'd always heard about him from John, of course. And then Tony moved to New York after his mother died. I was up at John and Marian's one weekend and so was Tony. And that was that."

"When was that?"

"Oh," said Lyle—as if he were trying to remember

some vague date in his life, not a turning point—"about ten years ago."

"So you were with Tony for ten years?"

"Nine," said Lyle. "He died last summer." Lyle paused. "He died up here, at John and Marian's." He nodded his head, once, in the direction that the train was traveling.

Robert did not reply.

"I'm sorry," said Lyle. "I shouldn't have said that."

"Of course you should," said Robert. "I want to know."

"Well," said Lyle, "it would be unfair, I think, if I didn't let you know what . . . the situation is."

"What else should I know?" Robert asked.

Lyle looked at him. "Oh," he said. "Lots and lots, probably. But most of it you know. The essentials, at least."

"Is it awkward, do you think, my coming with you this weekend?"

"No," said Lyle. "I'm very glad you're coming. I told you, if it weren't for you, I wouldn't be coming."

"I meant with John and Marian."

"I think they'll be very happy to see me with someone again. I'm sure they will."

"But this must be hard for you," Robert said.

"In a way. But in a way I'm very happy to be coming.

It's one of my favorite places on earth. And I don't want that to change. Ever. And I'm happy to be with you. I mean that." He wanted to reach out and touch Robert again, stroke the polished taut skin of his upper arm. But it was too self-conscious a gesture for Lyle to make, too deliberate, and expected. It was like a stage direction in a play: (*Touches Robert's arm*).

"What are they like?" asked Robert.

"Who?" asked Lyle, who had been staring intently at Robert's biceps.

"John and Marian. Their personalities."

"Well. Some people think John's rude or terribly shy, but he's not. Do you know how some people's personalities are larger than they are? Well, John's just the opposite. He doesn't quite extend all the way to the edges of himself. It takes patience and time to get to know him, but it's worth the effort. He's one of the most instinctively nice people I know. He's calm and decent and kind. He reminds me of you a little. I think you'll like him very much."

"And what about Marian?"

Lyle thought about mentioning Marian's skirmishes with depression, but he thought, no: that would be unfair. Marian, who had wandered some years ago into a dark valley and twice attempted to take her life, was better

15

now. She said so herself. So Lyle decided to describe the Marian he hoped that they would find. "Marian is a wonderful person. She's funny, and charming, and smart. She's interested and interesting. And she's a true friend, a loyal friend."

The train was pulling into a station. The delft lady stood up and was trying to retrieve a carpetbag that was squashed into the overhead rack. Lyle got up and helped her. "Thank you," she said. She collected the rest of her bags and walked toward the front of the car. The train stopped.

"This isn't us, is it?" Robert asked.

"No," said Lyle. Out on the platform people greeted each other, embracing and laughing. It was a lovely day in the hot still center of summer. The delft woman put on a blue straw hat and sunglasses. She stood on the platform, her bags clustered about her feet, waiting. She extended her bare arms to either side of her, raised toward the sun, as if to warm them, or give a benediction. The train pulled away.

"They sound very nice," said Robert, "John and Marian. You're lucky to have such good friends."

"I know I am," said Lyle. "I would be lost without them."

3

Lyle's most recent book, *Neo This, Neo That: The Rise and Fall of Contemporary Painting*, had become, to his surprise, a big success. He had been invited to lecture to emerging artists at Skowhegan, an artists' colony in Maine: two days, two lectures, two critiques. After his first lecture, wherein he basically said that to paint without acknowledging that painting was a moribund art form was to deceive oneself, and art produced in self-deception was pointless, he was led through the painting barns and sheds, where the young artists stood about like cows, staring at him, daring him to speak. He began to think he might be murdered while he was there. His lecture the second day was to have been a continuation of the first: a sort of highlights of recent self-deceptive and indulgent painting. But only one person showed up the next morning: the young man who was scheduled to drive him to the airport at the lecture's conclusion. He was being boycotted. This fact seemed not to bother the people in charge; they thought his presence there had been a good catalyst for discussion. So Lyle got in the car with the driver, who was named Robert, and they drove an hour through the gloomy wilds of Maine in silence. Lyle was hovering on the border of sleep when the driver spoke.

"What?" Lyle asked.

"Your lecture," Robert said. "The one you were going to give today. What was it about?"

"Oh," said Lyle. "More of the same vitriol. About the curse of abstraction."

"Abstraction is a curse?" asked Robert.

"Yes," said Lyle, "finally. And I don't mean just in painting. I mean in all the arts. In literature and music. Perhaps not in dance, because of Balanchine. His genius allowed abstraction to reinvigorate the art. But in all the other disciplines abstraction has proved a dead end. A wall that artists have been beating their poor heads against for the better part of this century. I think if painting—indeed, if art in general—is to survive, let alone matter, it must become reconnected to life as we live it."

"Who's we?"

"People," said Lyle. "The man—or woman—in the street. Painting can't be just for painters. That's the problem with music. When any art form becomes a dialogue of artists talking to themselves, it loses its—well, it loses the thing that makes it vital. That connects it to the world."

"You don't think it is?" asked Robert.

"Not even remotely," said Lyle.

"Perhaps the failure is on your part," said Robert.

"What do you mean by that?"

Robert shrugged. "I mean maybe you're not connected to the life that people are painting about. Maybe you don't approach it with the right experience, and attitude."

"I don't subscribe to that notion," said Lyle.

"What notion?"

"That I, as the viewer, am in any way responsible for the work's failure or success. I think that is a terrible notion that abstraction, because of its deficiencies, has introduced to the world of art. I bring nothing to a painting. The job of the painting is to bring something to me."

"Do you like painting?" asked Robert.

"Of course I like painting. I like good painting."

"And what do you think is a good painting?"

"A painting I can bear to look at for more than five seconds."

"Only five seconds? That's all?"

"Well, you know what I mean. Five minutes, then. You're a painter, I presume?"

"Yes," said Robert. "You saw my paintings yesterday. At your crit."

"I don't remember. What did I say about them?"

"Nothing," said Robert. "You sort of glided by and nodded. Like the Queen."

"That probably means they're good. It's the good ones I nod at. What do you paint?"

"Landscapes, mostly," said Robert. "Contemporary landscapes."

"Well, that sounds harmless enough."

"You think of art in terms of its ability to inflict harm?"

"No," said Lyle. "Of course not. Why are young people nowadays so literal?"

"I don't know," said Robert. "Ask a young person."

Lyle looked at Robert, who was looking at the road unfurling itself in front of them. "I'm in an awful mood, aren't I?" he said. "I'm sorry. This weekend was just a bit unnerving."

Robert did not reply.

"Do you like it at Skowhegan?"

"I like being able to paint all day. To have the time to be an artist. Or pretend to be one. I don't have that luxury in New York."

"Why not?"

Robert shrugged. "I can't afford it."

"If you really are an artist, you can't not afford it," said Lyle.

"Thanks," said Robert. "I'll keep that in mind."

"I meant that to be encouraging," said Lyle. "Actually, I admire you very much. Trying to be an artist. To be painting now, at this point in time. It takes courage. To be a painter, to spend time making paintings, to think you can paint something that matters, that takes courage."

Robert did not reply. Lyle looked out the window. They were on a highway now, and it no longer looked like Maine. They could have been anywhere. They continued in silence, and arrived, finally, at the airport.

"We're early," said Lyle. "I suppose I'll get some lunch. Would you care to join me?"

To his surprise, Robert did. They had a not unpleasant lunch in the awful restaurant at the airport. Lyle drank three glasses of wine and got a little drunk and gave Robert his phone number and told him to call him when he returned to New York. To his surprise, Robert did.

They went to the movies one evening in July, and had dinner, afterward, in the garden of a restaurant.

"So," said Lyle, "how is the painting going?"

"It's not," said Robert. "I've had to stop."

"Why?"

"I lost my studio. Actually, it wasn't really mine."

"Whose was it?"

"This friend of mine. He went to Barcelona for the year and was letting me use it. But it turns out he wasn't paying the rent. When I got back from Skowhegan the locks had been changed."

"Well, can't you pay the rent?"

"No," said Robert.

"Why not?"

"Because I don't have the money. I can barely afford my apartment. In fact, I can't."

"I know a studio you could use," said Lyle.

"Really? Where?"

"Well, it's not really a studio. But it could be. How big is your work?"

"Not big."

"Well, I have a room in my house that's empty. It would make a nice studio. You could use that, if you'd like."

"You have a house?"

"A brownstone," said Lyle. "On Bank Street. It's stupid to have the room go to waste. Why don't you come have a look?"

"Tonight?" asked Robert.

"Well, sometime," said Lyle. He realized Robert assumed the studio was simply a pretext for luring him back to the apartment. He thinks I want to seduce him, thought Lyle. How pathetic I must seem. Yet this realization did not stop him from saying, "What about tomorrow night?"

"I work tomorrow night," said Robert.

"Then what about Wednesday?"

"O.K.," said Robert. "If you're sure."

"Yes," said Lyle. "I'm sure."

On the way home Lyle wondered if he did perhaps want to seduce Robert. It was hard to discern, for sex was a subject, like geometry, that Lyle had once learned and now assumed he'd forgotten. Occasionally Lyle masturbated, quickly and dispassionately, as if he were servicing a car. But his sense of desire was gone, an amputated limb, a vague, sometime achy memory, suggested rather than felt. But Robert's intimation that Lyle was interested in—and perhaps capable of—seduction made him feel less sure about what he did not presumably desire. It made him nervous, and all Wednesday, waiting for Robert to come, he felt a little anxious. He remembered Robert's face during the movie. It was like something drawn with luminous chalk in the dark, serene and engaged. Robert had small, beautiful, intensely colored features: dark black eyes that seemed perpetually surprised and alert, surrounded by their just-washed whiteness; thin dark lips pulled taut across fine white teeth. Beautiful faces usually become closed with awareness of their beauty, but Robert's was not. His face was like a gift he had not yet learned to withhold.

While he waited for Robert, Lyle decided to clean out Tony's study a bit, or at least have a look at it. Of all the rooms in the house, this had been the one that had been solely Tony's. Lyle had entered it rarely while Tony was alive and only once since his death. He stood outside the closed door for a moment. He wasn't sure what he expected to encounter inside: cobwebs and mold wouldn't have surprised him. But of course everything was as it had been, only dustier.

Lyle sat down at the desk. There was a pale green Post-it stuck to the blotter with the address of a hotel in Buenos Aires. Tony had had a successful career writing travel articles for magazines. There had been talk about selecting some of his "better" pieces and printing them, elegantly, as a memorial. Lyle was supposedly editing it, but so far he had done nothing. He began to sort through the piles of magazines that were stacked about the room, separating the ones to which Tony had contributed from the ones to which he had not. But he did not progress far, for he began to reread Tony's articles, trying to find in the familiar and trivial words some new, subliminal meanings. Lyle felt there must be things he did not know about Tony. Of course there were things he did not know about Tony, but while Tony was living, it did not seem that way. Tony had always seemed easy and uncomplicated—a little shallow. Lyle had thought the mourning of him would be intense, simple, therapeutic. But it was not: it lingered, uncooperative. Lyle thought the character of mourning should suit the object rather than the subject. And his mourning did not suit Tony.

Lyle read until it got too dark to read. When he tried to turn on the lamp, nothing happened. The bulb was dead. He sat for a while longer, not reading, while the darkness completed itself. Robert was supposed to come by at seven o'clock. Lyle knew it was later than that, but he did not look at his watch, because he did not want to know how late it was, how late it was getting. He did not want to know how certainly Robert was not coming. He sat there in the dark feeling a bitter disappointment fill him, slowly. Or it was not something filling him—it was something going away. Leaking. He realized how buoyed with hope and expectation he had been these last few days: he had thought his life might finally be about to change. How naïve I was, he thought, and how stupid. My life is not going to change. He felt sunk again in the deep center of his sadness, as if he had made no progress in his mourning of Tony. Lyle had thought mourning would progress mathematically, a gradual but perpetual diminution of sadness: a slow, sure journey. One left the beloved city and watched it shrink in the distance until it disappeared, gone but remembered, faintly and fondly. But Lyle's journey was not like that: he found himself again and again clutching the closed gates of the empty city.

He looked at his watch. It was twenty past nine.

He went out to dinner to a not-very-good and consequently uncrowded Chinese restaurant around the corner. He had never been there with Tony but went there often, now, alone, and the people were nice to him. It was the kind of restaurant frequented almost exclusively by solo diners: hushed and dim and expectant, like a waiting room, where one could feel I am not really here, this is not my destination, I am only passing through. I am on my way somewhere else and there I will not be alone.

Lyle ordered a martini and sat drinking it. Across the street, he could see the corner of an apartment building, and he noticed that between the second and third floors a frieze of deep blue and gold mosaics decorated the stucco wall. He had never noticed them before, and could not understand what they were doing on such a nondescript, ugly building. He sat and looked at them. No one ever saw them, he was sure; they were at such an odd height. He looked at them and wished he could somehow let them know they were being looked at. The human effort to create beauty suddenly seemed to him useless and pathetic, and the pathos of it, as augmented by his almost-finished martini, was bottomless and overwhelming.

I need to change my life, he thought. It is unbearable. He was about to cry, but was saved from such embarrassment by the arrival of his dinner, which he heard approaching. The food at this restaurant was all served loudly sizzling, as if the drama of its presentation compensated for its mediocrity.

He was back in his own study, reading an article Tony had written about the carnival in Rio—no subliminal messages there—when the doorbell rang. He looked at his watch: it was a little past midnight. He decided to ignore it, but he found his concentration disturbed, so after a few minutes he went into the front bedroom and looked out the window toward the stoop. Robert stood at the top of the steps, looking down at the street. He was dressed very simply in black pants and a white dress shirt.

He stood there awhile, and then turned around and approached the buzzer, which he studied instead of pressing. Then he stepped back and looked up at the windows, and saw Lyle.

"Hey," he called, softly. "Were you sleeping?"

"No," said Lyle. "You're a little late."

"I know," said Robert. "I came to apologize."

"Would you like to come in?"

"Is it O.K.? I know it's late."

Lyle answered by ducking his head back in the window. In a moment he was unlocking the front door. The parlor floor of the brownstone was one large room with windows facing both the street and the garden. A living room in the front gradually transformed itself into a kitchen as it neared the back. "Sit down," Lyle said. "You look hot. Can I get you something to drink?"

"Just some water, please," said Robert. He sat on a large leather sofa.

Lyle filled two large glasses from the kitchen tap. He handed Robert a glass and sat in a chair opposite the sofa. "So," he said, after they had both drunk some water, "you came to apologize."

"Yes," said Robert. "I'm sorry I didn't come by this evening. I had to work tonight after all, so I couldn't."

"You could have called."

"I was going to, but I lost your number."

"I was sure you had changed your mind," said Lyle. "I was sure I'd never see you again."

"No," said Robert. "I'm sorry. Things just got messed up tonight. They changed the schedule at the last minute."

"Are you a waiter? You look suspiciously like one."

"Yes," said Robert.

"Where?"

"In an Indian restaurant."

"On Sixth Street?"

"Yes."

"Which one?"

"Agra."

"I don't think I've ever been there."

"You're not missing anything."

"Are you Indian?"

"I'm half Indian," said Robert. "My father is Indian."

"And your mother?"

"She was American, but she's dead."

"I'm sorry," said Lyle.

"She died a very long time ago. When I was a baby." Robert sipped his water.

"Were you born in India?" Lyle asked.

"Yes," said Robert.

"And you grew up there?"

"Until I was fourteen. Then I moved to my grandparents' in Wilmington."

"That must have been a shock."

"Actually, I wasn't very happy in India, with my father. So it was O.K."

"Were you happy in Wilmington?"

Robert laughed. "No," he said. "But I'm happy now. I'm happy in New York. At least I think I am."

"Except that you need a studio," said Lyle. "Should we go up and take a look?"

"I could come back," said Robert, "if it's too late. I really just came by to apologize."

"And you have. And I've forgiven you." Lyle stood up. "So let's go look at the room. It's upstairs," he said. "This way."

They climbed the narrow, curving staircase, and then Robert followed Lyle down a hall toward the back of the building.

"Here we are," Lyle said. He opened a door and switched on the light but the room remained dark. "Oh," he said, "I forgot. The bulb's dead. Well, go look. I'll try to find one."

Robert entered the hot room. It was small, and crowded with a desk piled with magazines and books and papers, and a sofa piled with more magazines and books and papers. A globe, as large as a medicine ball, stood on a floor stand. Robert tried to make it turn but it was stuck. A large casement window overlooked the trees in the back garden. Robert opened a window and leaned out. Below him people were eating dinner in one of the gardens. He could hear their talk and laughter and the clink of their cutlery, but he couldn't see them, so dense was the intervening foliage. Robert had not realized that there were gardens behind brownstones. He had assumed that all buildings in the city were divided, like his own, by air shafts.

Lyle returned with a lightbulb. He held it in his hand like a curiosity. It was frosted a soft, seashellish pink. "Let's try this," he said. He removed the brown paper shade from a lamp on the desk and unscrewed the bulb, replacing it with the new one. A rosy light warmed the room. Lyle looked around. "Goodness," he said, "what a mess." He picked up some piles from the sofa and then stood with them, as there seemed to be no place else to put them. "Here, sit down."

Robert sat on the sofa. Lyle continued to stand, holding the stack of magazines. "So what do you think?" he asked.

"It's not empty," said Robert.

"What?" asked Lyle.

"This room. You said you had an empty room, that you didn't use it. But obviously you do."

"Oh . . ." said Lyle. He looked around the room, as if its emptiness just had to be found. "You're right," he said. "But I don't use it. I meant we could empty it, if you wanted to use it for a studio. I would have done it myself, but I didn't have time."

"Why don't you use it?" asked Robert.

"It's not—it belonged to Tony," said Lyle.

"And it doesn't now?"

"No," said Lyle. He shuffled the magazines for a moment, as if looking for a specific one. "Tony is dead," he said.

"Oh," said Robert.

"He died last summer," said Lyle.

"He was your lover?" asked Robert.

Lyle nodded.

"I'm sorry," said Robert. He moved another pile of magazines from the sofa to the floor, clearing a spot beside him. "Sit down," he said.

Lyle sat down beside Robert. They were not touching, but Robert could feel the warmth from Lyle, and smell him. It was a natural, yet curious, odor: a sort of emotional perspiration.

"Was he a writer?" asked Robert.

"Yes," said Lyle. "Among other things. He wrote about travel. Very facile articles for stupid magazines. Blah blah blah blah don't drink the water." He tossed one of the magazines to the floor.

"Did you travel with him?"

"Sometimes."

Robert picked up the magazine. "I would love to travel," he said. "I think traveling is the most interesting and worthwhile thing you can do."

"Where would you like to go?" asked Lyle.

"I don't know. Just about anywhere. I want to go to South America. And Japan. And Europe, of course. Everywhere, basically."

Lyle had always maintained that traveling was a pointless and distracting activity. He did this mainly because it was something Tony had done: Tony traveled, and Lyle stayed at home, and so Lyle had come to dismiss traveling. You do not need to see the world to know it, he would say. Or traveling doesn't enrich you, it exhausts you. All sorts of bogus, pompous things. I was a bogus and pompous person, he thought. I am still.

"You seem tired," said Robert. "You should go to bed."

"I think I'm too tired to go to bed," Lyle said. "I'm

going to have a glass of wine. Would you like one? I'd offer you a beer, but I don't have any."

"Are you sure?" asked Robert. "I don't want to keep you up."

"Yes," said Lyle. "Please join me."

"O.K.," said Robert.

"I'll be right back," said Lyle. He reached out and touched Robert's head, and then went downstairs.

Robert opened one of the magazines. He was looking at a picture of the bludgeoned Berlin Wall when Lyle returned with two glasses of wine. Robert put the magazine down.

"So," said Lyle, "what do you think?"

Robert thought he meant the magazine. "It looks interesting," he said.

"I meant the room. As a studio. Of course, we would move all this out. It's really bigger than it looks. You'll see, when we get it cleared."

"But . . ." Robert began.

"But what?"

"Don't you want to—I mean, do you really want to move these things?"

"Yes," said Lyle. He handed a glass of wine to Robert, and took a sip from his own. "I should have done it ages ago. I've just been waiting for a reason. Now I have one.

At least I hope I do. You are a painter, aren't you? You do need a studio?"

"Yes," said Robert. "But . . ."

"But what?"

"It's just that it's . . . well, I'm not sure that it's right. I mean, I feel like I should pay you rent or something. You could probably rent this room for a lot of money."

"Perhaps I could. But I don't want to. I want you to use this room for a studio. Of course, if you don't want to use it, please tell me. I'm not going to force you."

Robert didn't know what to say, so he said nothing.

"I'm sorry," said Lyle, after a moment. "I get impatient sometimes, when people are being polite. It's very rude of me. I'm sorry." He got up and looked out the window. The dinner party was breaking up. A chorus of good nights floated up into the dark. He looked over at Robert, at the back of his head, at his dark sleek hair. He went over to the desk and turned out the light. A shadowed trellis of leaves and branches arched across the ceiling. He sat down beside Robert. He wanted to touch Robert again, but he didn't know how or where. So he raised his hand and made an odd gesture, as if he were holding some heavy object. "I'm sorry," he said.

"It's O.K.," said Robert. He sipped his wine.

They sat there for a moment, without talking. Lyle

reached out and put his hand on Robert's dark pants leg. Robert did not respond. He looked straight ahead, as he had at the movies, watching something.

After a moment Lyle said, "I'm tired."

"I'll go," said Robert. He put down his glass of wine.

"No," said Lyle, "I didn't mean—I meant: Are you tired?" He paused. "I meant, let's go to bed. I would like to sleep with you. Just sleep."

Robert was looking down at the floor, at his glass of wine. In the darkness he could just vaguely discern its color.

"Yes?" asked Lyle. "No?"

"Yes," said Robert.

Lyle stood up. "Tomorrow," he said, "we'll clear out this room."

Some birds on the windowsill woke Lyle. Robert was sleeping. He was turned away from Lyle, lying on his side, the sheet rising up over his legs and hip, his back and arms and head uncovered and beautiful in the soft morning light. Lyle lifted the sheet and peered beneath it at Robert's buttocks. They were paler than the rest of him, full, yet—even in sleep—taut. Lyle would have reached down and touched them but he was afraid it would wake Robert, so keenly would he have felt it himself.

Sleep veils some people; it takes them away. But sleep only stilled Robert; he lay there present and calm. There were no grinding teeth, no thrashing, no twitching, no groaning or snoring: it was an amazingly simple, peaceful sleep. It suggested to Lyle that if you unwound Robert like a wrapped mummy, you would find nothing bad, nothing rotten or broken or unnecessary, just everything, down to the bones of him, clean and perfect.

When Lyle got out of the bed the birds noisily erupted from the windowsill. This commotion stirred, but did not awaken, Robert. He turned over onto the part of the bed Lyle had vacated. Lyle watched Robert resettle himself. Then he got dressed and went downstairs.

He had made some coffee, and was sitting on the narrow wrought-iron terrace overhanging the garden, when the phone rang. He went into the kitchen and answered it.

"It's early, isn't it?" Marian said. "Did I wake you?"

"No," said Lyle.

"I had a feeling you were awake."

"I just got up. I was sitting out on the terrace, having coffee."

"I've just been for a swim."

"Lucky you," said Lyle.

"Yes," said Marian. "It was lovely."

"I'm looking forward to next weekend," said Lyle.

"That's why I was calling. To see when you were coming up. Can you make it on Friday?"

"I doubt it," said Lyle. "It will probably be Saturday morning."

"Well, I'm planning a little dinner," said Marian. "I should make it for Saturday, then?"

"Yes," said Lyle. "Who?"

"Her name is Laura Ponti. She's Italian. She knew John's mother. She's rented a house up here. We met her at a party the other night, and then I saw her again at the bookstore. The copies of *Neo This, Neo That* I ordered had come in, and when I went to pick them up, she asked me why I had ordered so many. She knew about you. And I said you were a friend. She seemed very interested, so I invited her to dinner."

"How many books did you order?"

"Five," said Marian. "So I'll tell her Saturday?"

"Yes," said Lyle.

"You'll like her, I think. She's very chic and intelligent. But come on Friday, if you can. Or come whenever. You haven't been up in ages. It's getting very boring up here in the country without you. You told me when we moved up here that you'd visit all the time."

"I've been so busy," said Lyle. "How's John?"

"I hardly see him. When he's not in the garden, he's building a stone wall in the meadow. He goes out in the woods with a wheelbarrow and digs up big stones and drags them back. It's a complete waste of time and energy, but it keeps him busy."

"He's not looking for another job?"

"No. He says maybe in the fall, but I doubt he will. If you don't need a job, and you don't like working, and you hate the city, what's the point?"

"One needs to be occupied."

"Well, this wall should keep him occupied for a couple of years."

"And Roland? How's he?"

"He's fine," said Marian. "He misses his godfather."

"Is he talking yet?" asked Lyle.

"Goodness, no," said Marian. "He's barely a year."

"Well, I wish he would hurry. I really prefer babies that talk."

"The thing about babies is that they don't talk," said Marian.

"Then I don't really get the point of them," said Lyle.

"You'll get the point of Roland when you see him," said Marian.

"How are you doing?"

"Fine. It's been a really lovely summer."

"You're feeling O.K.?"

"Yes," said Marian. "Better than O.K. Very calm and stable. Knock on wood." Lyle heard a faint knocking sound, and then a gush of Marian's laughter. "Oh, isn't it awful," she asked, "to aspire to stability? It's really pathetic, isn't it?"

"No," said Lyle, "not at all. I'm glad to hear you're doing well."

"The only thing that's wrong is my missing you. What have you been up to?"

Lyle heard the toilet flush and Robert descending the stairs. "Actually, lots," he said. "But I'll tell you next weekend, all right?"

"What? No, no, no. Tell me now," said Marian.

"No," said Lyle. "When I see you."

"Try to make it Friday, will you?"

"I'll try," said Lyle.

"All right. Have a good breakfast."

"You, too. Bye."

He hung up as Robert entered the kitchen. "Good morning," he said.

"Good morning," said Robert.

"Would you like some coffee?" asked Lyle.

"Yes," said Robert, "but I'll get it."

Lyle watched him get the coffee. He was wearing his black waiter pants and no shirt. "How did you sleep?"

"O.K.," said Robert. He stepped out on the terrace with his coffee. There was a woman sitting at a table in the garden below them, reading the newspaper. Most of the garden was paved with moss-mottled slate. Around its perimeters were beds of ivy in which stood copper urns full of lipstick-red geraniums. In the middle, near the woman, was a stone birdbath.

"Who's that in the garden?" Robert asked, stepping into the kitchen.

"Daphne," said Lyle. "She lives below me. She rents the basement apartment."

"Do you own this building?"

"Yes," said Lyle. "Now I do. It was Tony's."

"It's beautiful," said Robert.

"I know," said Lyle.

Robert stood by the terrace, studying the garden.

"Come here," said Lyle. He indicated his lap.

Robert considered a moment and then sat on Lyle's lap. Lyle wrapped his arms around Robert's chest and held him.

"Who were you talking to so early?" asked Robert.

"A friend of mine. She lives upstate. I'm going to visit her next weekend," he said.

"That sounds nice," said Robert.

"Does it? I suppose it does. I'm not really looking forward to it."

"Why not?" asked Robert.

"Oh, it's a long story. It's complicated." Lyle rested his chin on Robert's shoulder, so that his mouth was beside Robert's ear. "It was nice to sleep with you," he said. "Thank you."

"You're welcome," said Robert.

"I haven't slept with anyone in ages," said Lyle. "It's awful how nice it can be."

"Why awful?" asked Robert.

"Because then you miss it," said Lyle. He strummed Robert's bare chest, feeling for his nipples. "Would you do it again?" he asked.

"Sleep with you? Yes," said Robert. "I would."

Lyle waited a moment, his thumb reading, over and

over, the simple Braille dots on Robert's chest. "Would you sleep with me now?" asked Lyle.

Robert arched his back a little. "Now?" he said. "Yes."

4

John had made breakfast and was bringing it down into the garden. They had an old round table beneath the mulberry tree, which in the morning they dragged out into the sun. John had hung a bassinet from a limb of the tree, in which Roland was very content to have his naps.

Marian strode up the lawn from her morning swim. "Oh, good," she said. "I was hoping we could have breakfast outdoors. It's such a beautiful morning."

"Yes," said John, "one in a series." He was shaking the mulberry-stained tablecloth. It was damp and smelled of the night.

Marian took Roland out of his basket, which swung back and forth in the air, buoyed by his removal. He had been a weak and sickly baby yet everyone had said what a good baby he was—how little he cried, how content he was—but now as he got older his goodness and docility began to alarm Marian. Secretly she worried that perhaps he was not quite right in some way, although the doctor did not share her alarm: she told Marian to thank her lucky stars that she had a quiet baby. But Marian would have been delighted if Roland had screamed or thrown things. She spent hours with him, reading or singing or talking nonsense, and though he did not seem to get bored, he never seemed to be particularly engaged. Sometimes he would smile, faintly, as if he remembered something, from another life, that was amusing.

"What time did he wake up?" asked Marian.

"Just a while ago," said John. He replaced the cloth on the table, smoothing it out. "We should really get a new cloth. This one's a mess."

"It's fine for breakfast," said Marian. She put Roland back in the basket. A woodpecker clung to the tree trunk. "Look," she said to Roland, pointing: "bird." Roland looked. "Bird," she repeated. "Birdy."

"What?" asked John.

"There's a bird in the tree. A woodpecker, I think." John looked up. The bird flew away.

"Gone," said Marian. "Bye-bye."

"Are you going to take a shower?" asked John.

"Yes. But quickly. I'm starving."

"Will you bring the coffee out? And the paper, if it's come?"

"Yes," said Marian.

She went upstairs. Their bed was unmade and the room needed to be straightened. Later. She took off her nightgown, which was damp from her swim. From the bathroom window she looked down to see John feeding Roland. He was talking to the baby; she opened the window and leaned out to hear what he was saying but John heard her and looked up. He stopped talking. She waved and shook her nightgown out and draped it over the windowsill. As she got into the shower she could hear the telephone ringing down in the kitchen.

When she came back out with the coffee, John was digging weeds from the lawn. He had a pronged tool to assist him, and the vehemence with which he drove this into the ground often concerned Marian. Roland was crawling about the lawn beside his father.

"Did you get the telephone?" asked Marian.

"Yes," said John. "It was Lyle."

"What did he want? He's still coming, isn't he?"

"Yes," said John. He sat up on his haunches and pulled his shirt off. He threw it toward the baby. It landed on top of Roland's head, shrouding him. He stopped crawling. "See if he takes it off," said John.

"No," said Marian. "You frightened him." She lifted the shirt from Roland's head. He looked up at her. "There you go," she said. "Daddy's shirt."

"He's bringing someone," said John.

"Lyle?" asked Marian.

"Yes," said John.

"He's bringing someone? For the weekend? Who?"

"He didn't say. A friend, he said."

"He just called up and said he was bringing a friend?"

"No," said John. "He asked if it would be all right. And I said of course."

"What friend?" asked Marian.

"He didn't say."

"Did he ask for me to call him back?"

"No," said John.

"He didn't mention anything about a friend when I spoke to him last Thursday."

"Well, maybe it's a new friend. Maybe he just met him."

"It's a man?"

"I'm not sure," said John. "Yes, I think he said he."

"Why would he bring some man he just met here? Don't you think it's strange?"

"I didn't say he just met him. Maybe it's an old friend."

"Yes, you did. You said he just met him."

"Well, I got that impression. I could be wrong. It's probably an old friend."

"But we know all of Lyle's old friends. He wouldn't refer to an old friend as a friend. And . . . well, Lyle comes here to get away from his friends. He wouldn't bring one with him."

"Well, he is," said John. "Tomorrow on the 11:40."

"This . . . this messes everything up."

"What does it mess up?"

"I had invited Laura Ponti to dinner."

"Who's Laura Ponti?"

"Don't you remember? That Italian woman we met at Derek and Granger's. She said she knew your mother."

"That old lady?"

"She wasn't old," said Marian. "She was very interesting. And she was eager to meet Lyle, so it was all just perfect."

"So what's the problem now?"

"Well—now it will be five, instead of four, with this mystery friend of Lyle's."

"And what's the problem with five? It's not as if you were trying to set up Lyle with the old lady."

"That's not even funny," said Marian. "No, it's just that—well, there's a difference between four and five. Four is intimate, and five isn't. Everyone knows that."

"I don't," said John. "I really don't see the problem."

"Oh, it's not a problem. It's just—odd. It's very odd. For Lyle to call up like this and say he's bringing someone. I don't understand it. I wanted everything to be perfect this weekend, too, because . . ."

"Because why?"

"Because . . . do you know what this weekend is?"

"No," said John.

"It's the anniversary. Of Tony's death."

"Oh," said John.

"And that's why I wanted to have Lyle out for a quiet weekend."

"Well, I'm sure it will be a quiet weekend. It's no big deal. Lyle's just bringing a friend. You should be happy."

"Do you think he remembers?"

"What?"

"About the anniversary."

"Of course," said John.

"Why? You didn't."

"Tony wasn't my lover."

"He was your brother," said Marian.

"Yes," said John. "He was." He inserted his weeder into the ground and stood up. "Let's eat," he said. "Did the paper come?"

"I forgot to check," said Marian. "I'm going to call him."

"Lyle? What about breakfast? You said you were starving."

"I am," said Marian. "I'll be right back."

"What do you think I should do about beds?" Marian asked John that evening. They were in the living room: John was reading the newspaper on the sofa; Marian was sitting on the floor, folding laundry. Insects skidded across the ceiling and threw themselves at the light bulbs.

"About what?" asked John. He spoke through the scrim of newspaper.

"Beds," said Marian. "Beds for Lyle and his friend."

"I don't know," said John. He finally put the paper down. "What do you mean, what should you do?"

"I mean," said Marian, "are they sleeping together? Should I make up one bed or two?"

"Two," said John. "And leave it to them." He returned to his lair.

"In different rooms?"

"I don't know," said John. "No. The same room should be fine. Put them in the yellow room."

Marian watched him for a moment, and then said, "He never called me back."

"Perhaps he's been out all day. What time is it?"

"It's ten," said Marian. "Twenty past. Maybe I'll try him again."

John did not respond.

"Do you feel all right?" asked Marian.

"Yes. I feel fine." He didn't lower the paper but peered around one side. "Tired."

"I don't," said Marian. "My stomach feels odd. I wonder if it was the fish."

"Come here," said John. He patted the couch beside him. "Lie down."

Marian went over and lay on the couch with her head on John's lap. He was wearing a pair of shorts that smelled of sweat and the garden. His face was once again hidden by an awning of newspaper.

"Put the paper down," Marian said. "Please."

"Just let me finish this," said John.

Marian waited. Finally he folded the newspaper and tossed it on the floor. He turned out the light. He stroked the hair off Marian's face, gathering it into a tight coil. "You're upset," he said, as if he could feel it through her hair.

"Yes," said Marian.

"Things are bound to change with Lyle."

"I know," said Marian.

"You shouldn't let it upset you," said John.

"It's not a matter of letting," said Marian.

John dropped the coil. Marian felt her scalp relax. She reached up into the dark for John's hands, and found one. She held it with both of hers, felt it, as if it were an object she was trying to identify. Then she placed it on her forehead.

"I'm worried about something else, too," she said.

After a moment John asked what. It was a strange suspended moment, a moment like skidding in a car, the world turning around and around slowly and quickly all at once, the horizon losing its grip. But John's *What* stopped it.

"I'm worried about Roland."

"The doctor says not to worry," said John.

"Doctors can be wrong," said Marian.

"Yes," said John.

"I shouldn't have had a midwife," said Marian.

"What do you mean?"

"I should have had him properly, in a hospital."

"Why?" asked John. "It was fine. Everything went fine."

"No," said Marian. "I don't think he got oxygen quickly enough. He was turning blue."

"She said that was normal."

"I think she was lying."

"I don't think we should let ourselves think like this. The doctor would know, Marian, if anything was wrong. She would know, and tell us. The more you worry, the worse it seems, and gets. You've got to relax with him. He was very funny with me at bedtime."

"Was he?" asked Marian. She sat up. "How funny?"

"He didn't want me to put his pajamas on. He was kicking his feet and laughing."

"Was he really laughing?"

"Yes," said John.

"You should have called me," said Marian.

"I know this sounds weird," said John, "but I understand him in a way. I mean, I think he's fine. I do. He's just shy. He's reserved, like his father."

"I can't bear it," said Marian. "All these reserved men."

"Well, Lyle is coming tomorrow," said John. "That should liven things up."

"I'm going," said Marian. She was standing by the garden fence. John, who was on his hands and knees, weeding, didn't respond. She repeated herself, more loudly.

John looked up suddenly and said, "What?"

"I'm going to pick up Lyle. Do you want me to leave Roland with you or take him?"

"Why don't you take him?"

"All right," said Marian. "It means I have to move the car seat."

"Then leave him here."

"You'll keep an eye on him?"

"Of course I will. You like to help Daddy garden, don't you, Roland?"

Roland did not reply. Marian lowered him over the fence, onto the ground inside the garden. He crawled toward his father.

"You'll stop at the liquor store?" John asked.

"Yes," said Marian. "What did you decide about beer?"

"You might as well get a case, so we have it."

"What kind?"

"I don't know," said John. "Bass, or something."

"I thought I'd stop at Elmer's and see if they have any tuna or swordfish, and we can grill it."

"That sounds fine," said John. "You'd better go. You don't want to miss the train."

Marian looked at her watch. "I've plenty of time. Darling?"

"Yes?"

"You won't hide in the garden all afternoon, will you?"

"I don't hide in the garden," said John. "I work in the garden."

"I know. But not this afternoon, all right?"

"Of course not," said John. "I'm looking forward to seeing Lyle. When I'm through in here, I'll get out the croquet set. It's in the basement, isn't it?"

"It should be," said Marian. "We didn't play at all last summer."

"No," said John.

"I'm off, then," said Marian. "Wish me luck."

"What do you need luck for?"

"Oh, I don't know. I just want everything to go well."

"If you want it to go well, it will," said John.

"Are you sure?" asked Marian.

"Yes," said John.

"The weather's perfect." Marian looked up at the sky.

"See? I told you."

"But I don't control the weather."

"You don't? I thought you did."

"Get up." Marian motioned with her hand. "Come here."

John got up and walked to his side of the fence. "What?" he said.

"Nothing," said Marian. She kissed him, then lay her face on his shoulder. John extended his arms around her, but kept his hands in the air, for they were dirty, and Marian was dressed all in white. He kissed her neck, and then moved his mouth from her jaw to her shoulder. He kept his lips there, in the hollow above her collarbone. "I love you," he told her, because it was true and because he knew it was what she wanted to hear.

5

Laura Ponti was sitting by the pool, waiting for her daughter, Nina, to arrive, and watching one of the female gardeners pick mulberries off the flagstones. The gardeners came with the house, which she had rented for the summer. Her villa, outside Florence, was being renovated, and she had decided to spend the summer in the States, to be near her daughter, who was making a movie in New York. Nina was an actress. She got a lot of roles in what she referred to as "action pictures"; roles in which she invariably bared her breasts.

Nina had tried to persuade her mother to rent a house in the Hamptons, but Laura refused. She didn't particularly like the ocean, and she definitely didn't like the way Americans behaved when they congregated near it. They tried to be sensual and decadent, two things to which, in her opinion, Americans were not well suited. So she had told the realtor: just a nice house upstate; and that is what he had found her: a brand-new house, modern, with glass walls and decks and a pool, all surrounded by woods. The people who had built it didn't have the money anymore to live in it. That was another thing Americans seemed to have trouble with: living within their means.

The pool was for Nina, an alternative ocean, but she had yet to use it. Every week she called and said they had to reshoot over the weekend so she wouldn't be able to come up. Nina was in a movie about a serial killer who raised pigeons on the roof of his apartment building. Nina played a prostitute. Nina was thirty, and ever since she was twelve, and had been sent to boarding school in the States, Laura had lost the sense of being her mother. Not that she had ever been particularly maternal. Nina had always been precocious and independent; she had never seemed especially interested in having a mother, and Laura had to admit that being a mother had always bemused her. When Nina was away at school, friends would ask how she was doing, and Laura would think: Oh, yes, Nina. I have a daughter. She never felt she neglected

Nina, for you cannot neglect someone who does not desire or elicit your care. Now, as adults, they had a strange, tentative relationship: like old friends grown apart, feigning affection for old times' sake.

"Why don't you sweep them up?" Laura called to the gardener. The names of the gardeners were Margaret and Evie, but she wasn't sure which was which. Who was who. They were lesbians, she had been told. They lived half the year up here and half the year in Palm Beach, where they also tended gardens and pools. Normally, Laura ignored people who worked for her, but technically the gardeners were employed by the people who owned the house, and besides, she was bored. It was odd that she was bored this morning: she had been alone pretty much all of the summer, and yet she had never been bored. It was the waiting for Nina, the anticipation, that bored her.

The gardener, who was squatting on her haunches, looked over at her. "They'll burst," she said, "and stain the slate."

"Oh," was all Laura could think of to say. There really was a reason for everything. But no, she thought, that's not true. I just happened to ask a question for which there was an answer; it's wrong to conclude there's an answer for everything. There isn't an answer for everything. In fact, I'm sure there isn't an answer for far more than there is an answer for. She looked at the gardener and was wondering if there was something else she could ask her, if there was a way to turn this exchange into a conversation, when she heard a car in the driveway. She stood up, but then she felt foolish standing up, waiting, so she sat back down. "Will you go around front and tell my daughter I'm back here?" she asked the gardener.

The gardener scowled at her. She tossed her handful of mulberries into a silver bucket and wiped her stained purple hands on her shorts. She stood up and walked around to the front of the house.

Oh, please, thought Laura, don't give me that. I should think it would be a nice break from picking up berries. She wondered if this mulberry thing was a scam; perhaps the gardeners were just collecting them and selling them to the farm stand. Maybe I should ask for the bucket when she's finished. But what would I do with them? Did one eat mulberries? Or make wine from them? No, that was elderberries.

Nina appeared around the side of the house. She was followed by two men and the gardener. Nina was dressed in tight jeans, a man's sleeveless T-shirt, and high heels. She looked like a beautiful prostitute. Laura thought perhaps she was trying to stay in character, but deep down she knew her daughter was cheap.

"This place is impossible to find!" Nina said, as she approached. "And it's so far away! It took forever to get here. What time is it? Hello, Mother." She put her hand on Laura's shoulder and kissed her on both cheeks. "This is Anders—" She pointed to one of the men, a tall, good-looking man in a rumpled, dissolute sort of way. "And this is Jerry. Jerry drove us up—I decided not to rent a car, I thought it would be cheaper to hire a limo, but I'm afraid it wasn't. It was much farther than I thought. So we owe Jerry some money."

"How much?" asked Laura.

"One hundred," said Nina. "And I told him he could have a swim. God, the pool looks great!"

"I didn't know you were bringing someone," Laura said. She was up in her bedroom, counting out one hundred dollars from her purse. Nina was sitting on the bed. "You're lucky I went to the bank yesterday. Here," she said, handing the money to Nina.

"What about a tip?" said Nina. "Shouldn't we tip him? He's got to drive all the way back to the city."

"I should think one hundred dollars included the tip," said Laura.

"Mother, give me a twenty. I'll get reimbursed from the production company. They cover expenses like this."

Laura withdrew another twenty-dollar bill. She knew she would never see this money again. She didn't mind throwing money away; she just minded throwing it away on Nina. "You didn't tell me you were bringing a friend," she repeated.

"I know," said Nina. She went over to the window and looked out at the pool. Jerry was doing the dead man's float in the deep end. "I didn't know until this morning. I just felt sorry for Anders. He's Dutch, and it's his first film in New York, and he didn't have anywhere to go this weekend. Everyone was going away. And you said the house was big." She turned away from the window. "It's nice, the house. Do you like it?"

"It's fine," said Laura, "for a summer. But it has that awful renty feeling."

"What do you mean?"

"You can tell they came through and took every decent thing out of it. I had to go buy some cotton sheets and crystal. They had plastic wineglasses."

"It's pretty, though," said Nina. She turned away from the window. "Where do I sleep? Anders can sleep with me. We're—well, we're sleeping together. He's really very nice. He's Dutch. Let me go give Jerry his money, and get rid of him. Then we can have lunch. Have you eaten yet?"

"No," said Laura.

"It's really lovely here. It's a bitch to get to, but it's beautiful."

They ate outside, at an umbrella-shrouded table, beside the pool. Jerry and the mulberries and the gardener were gone, and Laura had relaxed a little. She didn't like it when being with Nina made her act ill-humored and disapproving; it made her feel old and rigid, which was not how she saw herself, and she resented her daughter for eliciting those qualities in her. So she willed herself to relax.

"Are you an actor?" she asked Anders.

"No," said Anders. "I'm an animal trainer. I train the pigeons."

"Anders can get a pigeon to do just about anything," said Nina. She had pushed her chair back from the table, into the sun.

"Do you work only for movies?" asked Laura.

"Now, yes," said Anders.

"He did the dogs in *Paws*," said Nina.

"I didn't see *Paws*," said Laura.

"Yes, you did. At least you told me you did. It was the one about attack dogs run amok."

"Do you specialize in violence?" asked Laura.

"Action," said Anders.

They're all such hypocrites, thought Laura: they make violent movies and call them action films. "But by action don't you mean violence?"

"Oh, Mother," Nina said, "they're just stupid movies. It's entertainment. For teenagers. Do you have any sunblock?"

"No," said Laura.

"God, I should have brought some. I'm not supposed to get any sun. I'm supposed to be a very pale prostitute." She lit a cigarette and went over to the pool, where she sat on the first of the tiered steps that descended into the shallow end. "So what's it like up here? What have you been doing?"

"Not very much of anything," Laura said. She was watching Anders peel green grapes with a penknife before eating them. While she generally admired people who peeled their fruit, removing the skin from grapes seemed a little excessive. He worked at each grape carefully and intently, and then popped it into his mouth quickly, as if the moist flesh might be damaged by prolonged exposure to the air.

"Have you been working on your book?" asked Nina.

"A little," said Laura. "Arranging my notes."

"You are writing a book?" asked Anders.

"About my late husband," said Laura, "Ettore Ponti. He was an architect." Actually, the book wasn't really turning out. She had spent the last year collecting his letters to friends and colleagues, only to discover—or perhaps confirm—what a profoundly boring and uninteresting man he had been. It had all seemed very different when she was giddy with widowhood.

"One of your late husbands," said Nina.

"My latest husband," Laura clarified.

Anders offered her a peeled grape. He held it out, pinching it between his thumb and forefinger. In the sunlight, it looked a bit like a large, uncut gemstone.

"No thanks," said Laura.

"And you're having your house in Italy remodeled?" he asked.

"Yes," said Laura. "I'm trying to bring it into the twentieth century, while there's still time. The plumbing was rather ancient."

Nina had waded into the pool. "I hope you're keeping

the fixtures. And I hope there's not too much chlorine in the water," she said. "Otherwise, I'll get a rash. How far is it to Woodstock? Somebody told me there's a good restaurant there."

"About forty minutes," said Laura. "Which one?"

"I don't know. Chez something. Do you want to go? Or should we cook something here? Is there a barbecue?"

"I'm going out tonight," said Laura.

"Where?"

"To a dinner. If I were sure you were coming, I would have asked for you to be invited, but I think it's a little too late for that now."

"With who?" asked Nina.

"A couple I met at a party. I knew the man's mother. Do you remember Iris Kerr? That beautiful American woman with all the money who lived in Rome and was such a drunk? It's her son. He's living up here with his wife."

"Tony Kerr? He's married?"

"No. Not Tony. This is the American son. His name is John."

"I wonder what ever became of Tony. He broke my heart."

"How?" said Anders. "When?"

"Oh, it was ages ago. When we were children. We went to Morocco together."

"You never went to Morocco with Antony Kerr," said Laura.

"Yes, I did," said Nina.

"When? How old were you?"

"Oh, I forget," said Nina. "Young. About eighteen, I think. I was madly in love with Tony. He was the most gorgeous man I've met. He liked boys, though."

"That's the way with so many beautiful men, I'm afraid," said Laura. "It's disheartening."

"What's this brother like?" asked Nina.

"He's a half brother. He doesn't make much of an impression—he was rather silent. Good-looking, though. I spoke with his wife, who isn't silent: she gushes."

"If they're so awful, why are you having dinner with them?"

"They're not awful," said Laura. "Besides, one takes one's society how one can get it. Especially in the hinterlands."

"But we're here," said Nina. "You have Anders and me tonight."

"I have you this afternoon and all day tomorrow. Tonight I want to go out. You'll have to forgive me if I don't tailor my plans to your schedule, Nina. You've hardly been reliable this summer."

"Well, then Anders and I will go to Woodstock."

"You won't have a car," said Laura.

"Oh," said Nina. She stood in the pool, moving her palms gently over the water's surface. "We'll stay here, then," she said. She looked at her mother for a moment —an odd, calm look betraying neither anger nor disappointment, but a look, Laura knew, intended to convey judgment—and then dove into the water.

6

Tony died on the last day of July. It was raining. He had been at Marian and John's house for about ten days, staying in bed, getting weaker and weaker, but not approaching death. Or of course approaching, but death seemed still a long way off. Tony refused to go back to the city and the hospital. He wanted to die at John and Marian's.

On the day Tony died, although she did not know it was the day Tony would die, Marian had left the house in the morning to buy some groceries. She was eight months pregnant. John was in the city, for he still worked then. Lyle was sitting with Tony.

As Marian drove toward town, the rain stopped and the sky lightened. She pulled off the road. There was a trail here, she knew, that wound down through the woods to a stream. She felt she needed a moment alone.

In the woods it was dripping, but the ground was dry. She stood for a while on the bridge of logs that lay across the swollen stream, watching the water gush furiously beneath her. She stood there until the rain started again and then she moved off the bridge and under the cover of trees. The sound of the rain and the stream seemed unnaturally loud. Not unpleasant, just forceful. All that water pouring through the world.

When she drove back up to the house, she thought it looked different somehow: closed, and empty. And then she saw Lyle sitting on the stoop, the front door shut behind him, and her immediate thought was *he's locked himself out*. She put the car in the garage but left the groceries in it and walked around front. Lyle didn't get up.

"What are you doing out here?" she asked. "What's wrong?"

"It's Tony," he said.

"What?"

"He died," Lyle said. "He's dead."

She wanted to ask him if he was sure but she knew she couldn't. But in a way she didn't believe him. So she asked. "You're sure?"

Lyle looked at her. His face was so wet with rain she couldn't tell if he had been, or was, crying. "He stopped breathing," he said. "And his heart isn't beating." He choked a little and then there was no doubt that he was crying.

"Come inside," she told him, almost fiercely. She helped him up and opened the door. In the foyer she held him, as best she could against her swollen stomach, and felt and heard him cry. She hadn't closed the door and she looked outside, at the rain pelting the dark wet grass and the huge, thousand-leaved trees. People shouldn't die in summer, she thought, not when the world is this ripe. She held Lyle, who cried for what seemed like a very long time. She almost forgot what had happened, so disorienting was it to be holding Lyle in the foyer with the door wide open. After a while they sat on the bottom step of the front stairs. She got up and closed the door. There was a puddle of water on the stone floor.

"We should call John," Marian said. "And the police, I suppose. Or the ambulance. I don't know, who should we call?"

"I don't know," said Lyle.

"I'm going to call John. Will you sit here?"

"I think I'll go back upstairs," said Lyle.

"Are you sure?" asked Marian.

"Yes," said Lyle.

"I'll be right up," said Marian. She went into the kitchen and called John. He said he would leave work immediately and get home as soon as he could. Marian sat for a moment at the table, with her head resting on her arms. Then she went up the back stairs. The door to Tony's room was closed. She thought: Perhaps I should stay downstairs longer, but she felt like something had to happen, and it was up to her. She knocked on the door. Lyle told her to come in. She opened the door. There were two beds in the room. They had arranged to rent a hospital bed but it had not yet been delivered. So in the room were two twin beds, two antique wooden beds, a pair. Tony lay on one bed with an arm hanging down over the edge, his head thrown back. His eyes were closed. The pillow was on the floor. Lyle lay on the other bed, the way Marian imagined dead people should rest: flat on his back, his hands crossed on his stomach, as if he were assuming Tony's death. She walked over to and opened a window. Then she sat down on the bed beside Lyle, put her hand on his.

"John is on his way," she said.

Lyle nodded.

"I think I should call the police," she said, "and find out what to do."

Lyle nodded again.

"Do you want a drink?" asked Marian.

"Not now," said Lyle.

Marian looked over at Tony. "Can I move him?" she asked.

Lyle looked at Tony. For a moment he didn't respond, and Marian was about to pretend she hadn't asked her question, but then Lyle said, "Yes."

She stood up and tried, gently, to untwist Tony's torso, model it after Lyle, but Tony's stiff doll limbs would not cooperate. She got him as flat as possible and then covered him with the blanket, smoothing it over him. She could not bring herself to cover his face, which she touched with her fingers. His hair was dirty. Marian and Lyle had intended to give him a shampoo that evening.

Lyle was sitting up, watching her.

"It was what he wanted," said Marian. "To die here. With you."

Lyle raised his shoulders toward his ears and shook his head, and then his whole body, in a sob-like way. "I don't know what he wanted," he said.

Marian sat down on the bed and held Lyle again while he cried. This time was shorter, and she thought: Every time now will be shorter, fewer and fewer tears until there are none. But she was wrong. The arc of Lyle's grief knew no pattern.

When he was finished crying this second time, Marian said, "I'm going to call the police now."

"Yes," said Lyle.

"Why don't you come downstairs with me, and have a drink?"

"I'll come down," said Lyle. "In a minute."

"O.K.," said Marian. It seemed an awful thing to say: O.K. How could you say O.K. with Tony, dead, in the room? But she said O.K. It was O.K. for Lyle to sit there, if he wanted, a while longer.

She went downstairs. Her call to the police set in motion a great deal of complicated activity that involved the rest of the afternoon and evening, for death is complicated. Looking back on it, she saw the moments she spent in the house alone with Lyle and Tony's body as the eye of a storm. There had been the awful activity of Tony's illness and the subsequent difficult period of his mourning, but those hours in between had been so quiet and still, as if a hush had settled on them, on her and Lyle and Tony, momentarily, and then been blown away.

7

"This is odd," said Lyle. "Usually she's here waiting." He and Robert stood in the parking lot of the train station, which, now that the train and the cars that had arrived to meet it had departed, was empty and quiet.

"Should we sit down?" asked Robert. There was an uncomfortable-looking bench, made from slabs of concrete, near the sidewalk where they stood. Beside it were several newspaper-vending boxes.

"No," said Lyle, rather abruptly, and then, upon hearing his tone, he added, "I want to stretch my legs." He began pacing, as if not to pace would prove him a liar. Robert sat on the bench and watched him. It was just beginning to feel hot. Robert stretched his bare legs into the sunshine, obstructing Lyle's route.

"Sit down," he said to Lyle. "Relax."

Lyle paced a little more just so it would not appear that he was taking orders from Robert, and then sat beside him. "You seem nervous," said Robert.

"I am," said Lyle.

"Why?"

"I don't know," said Lyle.

"I'm the one who should be nervous," said Robert.

"Why should you be nervous?" asked Lyle.

"About meeting John and Marian."

"But I just told you how friendly and wonderful they are. You have nothing to be nervous about."

"Then neither do you."

"Yes," said Lyle. "I suppose." He leaned back against the bench. He actually felt as if he might be sick. It's the train, he tried to tell himself, although he knew it was not. Nothing about who he was, or where he was, or whom he was with, or where he was going, felt right in and of itself, and the thought of him sitting here beside Robert waiting for Marian to pick them up and take them to the house suddenly seemed immensely foolish and frightening. He was wondering if there was time to cross the platform and take a train back to the city, when he saw a car pull off the main road and drive down the hill toward the station. It was Marian. He tried to say something but couldn't speak. So he pointed at the car.

Robert said, "Is that her?"

Lyle nodded and stood. He was aware of Robert standing beside him, of Marian stopping the car in front of them, and her jumping out from it. She looked so animated and joyful, and for a moment, in the delight of seeing her again after so long, Lyle forgot his fears. It is all going to be fine, he thought.

"Oh, I knew you'd be waiting!" Marian exclaimed. "I'm sorry I'm late. Have you been waiting long?"

"No," Lyle managed to say. "Not long at all. Marian, this is Robert. Robert, Marian."

"Hello," said Robert. They shook hands.

"We're so glad you've come this weekend," said Marian. She turned to Lyle. "And Lyle," she said. "You—" She hugged him hard, rubbed his back. "It's wonderful to see you. You look great."

Lyle could see Robert standing behind Marian, watching them embrace. He was smiling in a way that Lyle didn't understand, or care for, so he closed his eyes. Marian hugged him tighter, as if she had sensed he had closed his eyes, and he knew she had closed her eyes, too—it was a blind, tight hug—and then she pulled away.

They all got in the car: Lyle in front beside Marian, Robert in back with their bags. "We've got to stop at the fish market and the liquor store and then it's straight home," Marian said. "I hope you don't mind. Do you eat fish?" she asked Robert.

"Yes," said Robert.

"Good," said Marian. They were waiting for the stoplight. For a moment no one said anything. When they had pulled into the traffic, Marian said, "And how was the train ride?"

"Fine," said Lyle.

"Was it crowded?"

"Yes," said Lyle.

"I think it's such a lovely ride," said Marian. "It's one of my favorites, up along the river. Had you taken it before?" she asked Robert.

"No," said Robert.

"Have you ever been in this area?"

Robert said he had not.

"It's nice," said Marian. "Especially in the summer. It's a bit nowheres, so there's not a lot to do, but I don't mind that. It's easy enough to go down to the city if you want to do something. Although, now with Roland, that's become a thing of the past." She laughed.

"How is Roland?" asked Lyle.

"He's fine. He's home helping John with the garden. Roland is our son," she said into the rearview mirror. "He'll be one year old next month."

"Lyle told me," said Robert.

Marian pulled the car into the parking lot of a small shopping center and parked. "Listen," she said, "I'm going to just dash into Elmer's for some fish. Would you two mind going into Kroegstadt's there and getting some beer? Do you drink beer?" she asked Robert.

"Yes," said Robert. "I like beer."

"Good," said Marian. "Then get some kind you especially like. John said to get a case. Here's twenty dollars. Is that enough for a case? I've no idea."

"We'll pay for the beer," said Lyle.

"No, no, don't be silly," said Marian. "Here," she said to Robert, holding the money toward him. "Take this, will you? I insist."

Robert didn't know what to do. "Are you sure?" he asked.

"Yes," said Marian. "Please. I won't forgive you if you don't."

John was trying to lay out the croquet court despite interference from Roland, who crawled behind him, uprooting each wicket as soon as it had been inserted into the lawn. It was a game, John realized, a game Roland played seriously, only sometimes emitting a small hiccuping burst of pleasure. They played it for about twenty minutes, until Roland grew tired. Then John whacked a yellow croquet ball around the lawn, while Roland lay down on the other balls, as if he were trying to hatch them.

The croquet set had been a gift from Tony, who had been an excellent croquet player. He played a misleadingly casual game, swinging the mallet in one hand and holding a cocktail or a cigarette in the other, playing inattentively and recklessly until some moment late in the game when he would discard the drink or smoke and bring the game to a swift, and for him victorious, conclusion.

Poison! he would call out. Now I am poison!

John's mother had divorced his father and moved to Italy when he was five. John had stayed with his father in New York. Tony was born a year later. He had an Italian father who was, as his mother herself used to say, "never really in the picture." In the beginning John had spent several summers in Europe with his mother and Tony, but Tony had been just a baby then, so John had played alone at the Mediterranean resorts his mother frequented. After a summer or two of that, though, John's father had suggested he might like to go to camp and John had agreed. Camp Phoenicia was very different from Club Azul but John had liked the difference. He was aware of the difference, even then. Sometimes in the hot pine American woods he would catch a whiff of the cypressy smell of Italy and think: Tony and Mother are on the beach. I am not like that, he had told himself. And then he would think of his dad in New York with Florence (stepmother) and Susannah (half sister) and think: I am not like that either. I am here, alone, in New Hampshire, at Camp Phoenicia. In a way he had never lost that feeling of himself, for that had been the first moment he was aware of having a sense of himself, of having figured out who he was. And John felt he had not changed in any substantial way since then. The intervening years were a clear pool of water, and he could always look back through them and see, and recognize, that boy, alone, in the woods.

One summer Tony had been sent to Camp Phoenicia. By then John was a junior counselor. Tony hated camp. He hated everything about it: the bunks and the sports and the cold lake and the food and all the other boys. He shivered all the time, and said he couldn't get warm. He was sent home, all the way to Italy, after only two weeks. John felt as if he had failed: he was supposed to have looked out for his brother.

The experience was a sort of sundering, but it proved, in the long run, to be mutually beneficial. Tony went on to cultivate his personality, which was very different from John's, and John stopped trying to make Tony American, and masculine. For a while, as teenagers, they assumed they were opposites, not just different, and they had very little to do with one another. But as they got older and more complicated, the polar extremes they had so easily assumed grew uncomfortable and hard to maintain, and began to melt. As adults they found they were rather fond of, and fascinated by, one another.

John had whacked the ball down near the river when he heard Marian calling him from up near the house. She was holding Roland, and Lyle and a young man in shorts were standing next to her. They were all looking down the lawn toward him. Marian waved for him to come. He hit the ball as hard as he could and then chased it up the hill, passing it on the way.

"You've been practicing," said Lyle. "That isn't fair."

"Hey," said John, between pants. "It's good to see you." They embraced sincerely yet a little awkwardly, for they had never worked out the physical component of their friendship.

"This is Robert," said Lyle. "And Robert, this is John."

John and Robert shook hands. "Did you have a good trip?" John asked.

"Yes," said Robert.

"Look," said Lyle suddenly, pointing to the river. "There's the river."

"Yes," said Robert. "I see it." And then he realized that Lyle hadn't really been pointing out the river so much as eliciting a comment about it, so he said, "It's beautiful."

"Yes," said Lyle, looking around. "How's the garden?" he asked John.

"I think I've outdone myself this year," said John. "And I have to show you my wall."

"Well, let's see," said Lyle.

"Don't you want to come inside first?" asked Marian. "I should think you'd like to freshen up."

"I'm feeling very fresh," said Lyle.

"What about you, Robert? Why don't we bring your things inside and I can show you your room. And get you something cold to drink. You look parched."

"O.K.," said Robert.

"I'll be right in," said Lyle. "I just have to see this wall."

"Is the wall decorative or functional?" Lyle asked as he and John walked down the lawn.

"Why?" asked John.

"Why? What do you mean, why?"

"Why do you ask that question?"

"Because I want to know the answer," said Lyle.

"It's neither," said John. "As far as I can tell."

"Then what is it?"

"Maybe I should show you the garden instead. I don't think you'll understand the wall."

"What's there to understand?" asked Lyle.

"That there is nothing to understand."

"It sounds very Zen," said Lyle.

"It's this way," said John. He turned from the lawn and pressed himself between the fir trees that bordered it. It was hot and fragrant and unpleasant in the midst of the trees. On the other side of them was a small meadow Lyle had never seen, with some sort of grass that had grown so tall and thick it all fell over, backwards or forwards, like church fainters. A stone wall, about three feet high, curved across the meadow in the shape of an imperfect S. It was tapered, with large stones at the bottom and small stones—almost pebbles—on the top.

"See," said John.

Lyle began to walk around the wall. He picked some of the smaller, round stones off the top, palmed them, and returned them to their places. "Where did you get the idea for it?" he asked.

"I don't know," said John. "I just started building it and it happened this way."

"It reminds me of something," said Lyle.

"What?"

"I can't think. Something about its shape, and the way

that it defines the space. I'd like to see it from the air. How long have you been working on it?''

"Not long. Since the spring. March.''

"It's beautiful." Lyle had returned to John's side. "It's very druidic. We should come down here at night and perform some sort of ceremony.''

"What sort of ceremony?'' asked John.

"I don't know," said Lyle. "Something with candles and drums. We should be naked. I'm sure something would happen.''

They were silent a moment, looking at it. "I should go find Robert," said Lyle. "I think he's a bit nervous.''

"How long have you known him?'' asked John.

"Not long," said Lyle.

"How did you meet him?''

"I met him at Skowhegan," said Lyle. "He's a painter.''

"Oh," said John.

"We're changing Tony's study into a studio for him,'' said Lyle. He knew he was saying too much too soon, but it was important, he thought, to mention Tony. For if Tony was talked about, included, he wouldn't haunt them. "It seemed," he continued, "stupid to let the room go to waste.''

"Yes," said John. "Is he a good painter?''

"To tell you the truth, I've no idea, and I don't really care. I'm not interested in being his mentor. Besides, didn't you read my book? It's my theory that there can be no more good painters, since we have experienced the death of painting."

"I suppose that makes your job as a critic easier."

Lyle was looking at the wall. It cast an odd, curved shadow on the ground. "Do you think I shouldn't have brought him?"

"No," said John. "Of course not."

"Does Marian?"

"No," said John. "We're both happy you did."

They were silent a moment.

"How is Marian?" Lyle asked.

"She's good," said John. "Ever since we moved here, she's been fine. Well, except for Tony, of course."

"Yes," said Lyle.

"I don't know," said John. "How does she seem to you?"

"Good," said Lyle. "It's wonderful to see her."

"Yes," said John.

"And how about you?" asked Lyle.

"I'm fine," said John. "I like it here, too."

"It's my favorite place in the world," said Lyle.

"Then you should visit it more often."

"I intend to," said Lyle. "I needed a little time away from it, I think."

"We missed you," said John. He, too, was looking at the wall, as if that were the focus of his attention.

"I think your wall is beautiful," said Lyle.

They pressed themselves through the fir trees and walked up the lawn. The sun had swung high enough so that it struck the back of the house. The windows shimmered, and Lyle thought it had never looked more beautiful. Marian and Robert are somewhere in that house, he thought. But he could not imagine where they were, or what they could possibly be saying to each other.

"Parts of the house date from the eighteenth century," said Marian, as she led Robert up the stairs.

"Which parts?" asked Robert.

"Oh," said Marian. "Well, parts of the cellar, I believe—there's a what-do-you-call-it, a root cellar—and the fireplace in what was the parlor but's now the library. Do you know Derek Deitz and Granger Salomon?"

"No," said Robert.

"Well, they restore old houses. They've done quite a few up around here. This was one of the first they did. We used to just come up here on the weekends, but we moved here for good about two years ago." They had reached the second floor and paused for a moment, in a patch of sunlight on the landing. "The only thing that isn't authentic about the house are these skylights," Marian said, pointing above them to a paned window that was set into the sloping ceiling. "Derek and Granger almost sued me when I had them put in. But it was so gloomy up here, with the big trees so close to the house. And I can't stand a gloomy house."

She paused, and Robert was aware he was supposed to make some remark, but he was at a loss: no one liked a gloomy house. He smiled.

"I don't think they look so bad," Marian said. "At least they aren't those awful modern ones that look like bubbles. And you can't see them from the front. I had these especially made. I bought the windows at an auction and had a glazier reset them with tempered glass. But I think you can go too far with authenticity. I don't want to live in a museum."

"I've always thought it would be nice to live in a museum," said Robert. "They seem much nicer than homes."

"But they aren't homes," said Marian. "One should live in homes and visit museums."

"It depends on the home," said Robert.

Marian looked at him for a second, as if to discern if this remark was an observation or an attack. She could not tell. "I'm going to put you and Lyle in the yellow room. As a rule, I hate people who refer to rooms by their color, but it's something we seem to do in the house, since all the rooms are different colors. You might be interested to know that the colors are replications of the ones Jefferson used at Monticello."

"Oh," said Robert.

"If all this house talk bores you, let me know. For some reason this house just compels me to talk about it. I can be an awful bore, I know."

"No," said Robert. "It's interesting. It's a beautiful house."

Marian opened a door on the landing. "These are the back stairs," she said. "They go down to the kitchen, if you're looking for a shortcut. We keep the door closed, though, now that Roland is crawling."

"O.K.," said Robert.

"Your room is this way," said Marian, walking down the hall. The walls were covered with framed photographs of many sizes, some old, some new. Robert noticed they were all of people, people from different decades in different countries, all jumbled together. Marian saw him looking at them. "There's an awfully funny one of Lyle somewhere. Here it is." She pointed to a photograph of Lyle dressed curiously, in what looked like knickers and a blouson.

"Is he supposed to be a pirate?" asked Robert.

"No." Marian laughed. "He's supposed to be Lysander, from *A Midsummer Night's Dream.* We used to have a party every year on Midsummer night. People had to come as characters and we'd read the play outside. Lyle was always a very grudging participant. It's funny how some people who are inherently theatrical clam up when they have an opportunity to really act. I don't understand it."

Next to the photograph of Lyle as Lysander was a photograph of Lyle and another man standing in a desert beside a camel. A few pyramids interrupted the vacant horizon. The camel had moved its head, creating a blur, but the two men were standing still, looking straight at the camera, at Robert and Marian.

"Is that Tony?" asked Robert.

"Yes," said Marian. "They went to Egypt in—I guess it was '87. Lyle was trying to grow his hair long then. It looks terrible."

"Yes," said Robert.

Marian looked at him, as if he should not have agreed. She turned away from the photographs and said, "You can use this bathroom here." Robert looked in the room. It was larger than a normal bathroom. A claw-footed tub stood in the middle of the floor and there was an over-stuffed sofa against one wall. "It hasn't got a shower, but it has one of those hand things," Marian said. "I hope it won't be a nuisance."

"It'll be fine," said Robert.

"Watch your step here," said Marian, as she walked down two steps and opened a door at the end of the hall. The yellow room was small, with various sloping roofs and two dormer windows. The walls were painted a beautiful shade of yellow: soft yet bright, the color of real butter. The curtains and the spreads on the two beds were of the same material: pink and white peonies exploding across a pale yellow background. The windows were open, but the old-fashioned brown paper shades were drawn and sucked tight against the screens. Marian raised one and opened the window wider.

"It's hot in here now," she said, "but it cools off in the afternoon. I promise."

"What a nice room," said Robert.

"Oh," said Marian, "I'm glad you like it."

They stood there, in the warm yellow light. It was the first moment they shared that wasn't tinged with anxiety.

Neither of them could think of how to preserve or extend it, so they said nothing. Marian clapped her hands softly together in a gesture that might have seemed odd but didn't, and said, "Well, then. I'll leave you to settle in. I'd better go check on Roland, and see about lunch."

"Thank you," said Robert.

Marian turned at the door. She nodded, then smiled. "You're welcome," she said.

Since they were only staying overnight there was very little settling in to do. Robert put his bag down and stood in the room for a moment, then went into the bathroom and washed his face. He knew he should go downstairs and join Marian, or Lyle and John, whom he could see out the window, standing on the lawn, aimlessly swinging croquet mallets, but he felt a little paralyzed. Who is Lyle? he wondered. It was strange to see someone you have only known alone begin interacting with other people, for that somebody known to you disappears and is replaced by a different, more complex, person. You watch him revolve in this new company, revealing new facets, and there is nothing you can do but hope you like these other sides as much as you like the side that seemed whole when it faced only you.

8

By midday the heat had extended itself even into the shade. The air seemed embalmed. Marian had planned to have lunch outside, but they decided it was cooler to eat indoors, at the large, slate-topped table in the kitchen, with the fan on and the blinds all drawn.

"So you're a painter, John tells me?" Marian asked Robert, when the platters of pasta and chicken salad had been passed around.

"Well, that's what I'm doing now," Robert said. "Or trying to do."

"So you don't really think of yourself as a painter?"

"No," said Robert. "Not really."

"That's interesting," said Marian. "I always thought it was important for artists to have that strong sense of self-definition, because the world is so unencouraging. But perhaps artists today are more practical."

"I guess I think it's presumptuous. I just started painting a little while ago. I suppose I see myself as more of a student of painting than a painter."

"You were at Skowhegan?"

"Yes," said Robert.

"Then you must be a very good student."

"I don't know. It was kind of a fluke, my being there."

"I'm sure it wasn't," said Marian. "What do you think, Lyle? Did you think it a fluke?"

"I don't believe in flukes," said Lyle. Marian had the feeling he hadn't really been paying attention to the conversation.

"Speaking of flukes," said John. "Did you get any fish?"

"Yes," said Marian. "I got some swordfish. And I'm going to make that salsa marinade, so I'll need some cilantro from the garden." She was not going to give up on Robert that easily, however. "I'd like to see your work, sometime," she said to him. "Or don't you like people to see it?"

"No," said Robert. "I don't mind."

"That's good," said Marian. "I never trust those artists who won't show you their work. It seems to contradict the purpose."

"And what do you think the purpose is?" asked Lyle.

Trust Lyle, Marian thought, to become interested in the conversation once it had turned from the specific to the abstract.

"To communicate," said Marian.

"Do you think that there's a difference between visual art and literature in that respect?"

"Well, of course there's a difference. Visual art no longer communicates as directly as literature, but its purpose hasn't changed. Painting shows you one scene, from which you must infer the story. Literature tells the story."

"So you're talking only about narrative art?"

"Yes."

"But narrative art is dead."

"Oh, please," said Marian. "We've had this discussion before. Art forms don't die. They grow fatigued, and are reinvented. But I do know what you mean, and in that respect I think literature is just as fatigued."

"How do you mean?"

"I mean . . . Well, I mean that the world has changed in a way that precludes literature as we know it. I mean novels, and stories. Poetry, I think, is timeless. But novels —there's no reason to write novels any longer. The problems that are best solved in novels no longer exist."

"What problems are they?"

"Well, it seems to me that all the great novels dealt with one of a few things: the failure of marriage or the sublimation of homosexuality."

Lyle laughed.

"It's true!" said Marian. "If you think about it. And now that people get divorced—or don't even get married in the first place—and now that homosexuals can live openly and honestly, all the tensions that complicate great fiction cease to matter. So the domestic novel, as we know it, will—well, I think it's already happened. Do you read contemporary fiction?"

"Not if I can help it," said Lyle.

"You see? Neither do I."

"Why not?" asked Robert.

Marian looked at him. She had been enjoying this conversation with Lyle. They often talked intellectually and argumentatively when they got together, simply because they liked to, and no one else ever indulged them. So they indulged one another. What was said didn't really matter. It was the experience of saying it that they enjoyed. And Robert's simple question put an end to all of it. For Marian did read contemporary fiction, and if Lyle had asked the question she could have invented a perfectly good reason why she didn't, but lying to Lyle was different from lying to Robert. Lyle would know she was lying and Robert wouldn't, for one thing. And she wasn't sure she wanted Robert to think she was the kind of person who didn't read contemporary literature. So she looked at Robert for a moment.

He looked uncomfortable. "I mean, I don't read much fiction, but I don't think it's ceased to have a purpose. I agree that domestic life has changed, but that in itself is—well, a reason to continue reading and writing fiction. Although I guess nonfiction could explore those changes better than fiction."

Marian thought: If Lyle had said that, I would know what to say. I would say that fiction has always been able to express most clearly how society changes. What society is. But she wasn't sure she wanted to say this to Robert. It would mean verifying what he had said, including it, including him. It was better, she thought, to remain silent.

Lyle came to Robert's rescue. "Well," he said, "I think all art serves no purpose."

"Do you really think that?" asked Marian.

"I don't know," said Lyle. He tossed his napkin on the table. "In this sort of heat, I could convince myself I did."

"You couldn't convince me," Marian said. "And that's the whole problem with criticism," she added. "It's just smart, thwarted people like you trying to convince themselves of things."

"Is that how you see me: smart and thwarted?" asked Lyle.

"Is there more iced coffee?" asked John.

"No," said Marian. "Should I make some?"

"No," said John. "I think I'm going to return to the garden."

"But you promised me you'd keep out of the garden!" said Marian. "What about croquet?"

"It's too hot for croquet," said John. "We'll play croquet later."

"Then I would think it's too hot for the garden. How about a swim?"

"We'll swim later," said John. He stood up. "After croquet. I'll go get you that cilantro. What else do you need?"

"Tomatoes," said Marian, with a British accent. "And peppers. And we might as well add some zucchini."

"Robert," John said, "why don't you come with me? I can show you my garden, and then you can bring the stuff back to Marian."

"Not everyone in the world wants to see your garden," said Marian.

John looked at her. "Robert is not everyone in the world," he said.

He thinks I've said or done something wrong, thought Marian. But at least I've said or done something. At least I haven't sat there saying nothing and then excused myself to the garden.

"Do you want to come, Robert?" John asked.

Robert stood up. "Yes," he said. "I'll be right back."

"Oh, take your time," Lyle said. "I'll help Marian with the cleaning up."

"No, you won't," said Marian. "Why don't you go sit in the library? It's cooler in there."

"Because I don't want to go sit in the library. I want to help you," said Lyle. He began to stack the dishes and carry them to the sink.

John and Robert went out the door and down the lawn toward the garden. For a moment Lyle and Marian busied themselves with the task of clearing the table. Each of them hoped the other might speak first.

"You didn't answer my question before," said Lyle. "Do you really think I'm thwarted?"

"Of course not," Marian said. "I don't know what I was saying. I was just trying to make conversation."

"Why?"

"Why?" asked Marian. "I wanted to make sure it wasn't awkward."

"Why would it be awkward?"

"I don't know," said Marian. "I just thought it might be."

"Is it?" asked Lyle.

Marian was washing her hands with cold water. "Yes," she said. "A little." Out the window she could see John and Robert disappear through the hedge. And then it was just the long slope of lawn, and the river, and the sun stilling all of it. She was aware of Lyle behind her, wiping down the table, but she didn't turn around. "Of course it's awkward," she said. "I'm not going to pretend it's not. But there's nothing—I mean, it *should* be awkward. It's perfectly O.K. for it to be awkward."

"I don't see what's so awkward," said Lyle.

"You don't?" asked Marian. She turned around. "Really, you don't?"

Lyle stood with a fistful of crumbs, observing them carefully and idiotically. "No," he said.

"Do you know what this week is?" she asked.

"No," said Lyle. "What?"

"The anniversary. Tony died a year ago this week."

"I know that," said Lyle. "Of course I know that. But every day is an anniversary of his death."

"Perhaps I'm just sentimental," said Marian.

"We're all sentimental," said Lyle. "I'm sentimental."

"Well, it just seems odd, that you would do this."

"Do what?"

"Oh, I don't know," said Marian, thinking: I'm not going to pursue this. It will only create more trouble. But then she thought not pursuing it, not speaking, would be false, and the weekend, and her life together with Lyle, would continue as a charade. "No, I do," she said. "And so do you. What's odd is this: for you to not come all summer, and then come this weekend, and bring someone."

"But you know I've been busy this summer," said Lyle. "And we agreed on this weekend over a month ago. And then I met Robert. And I wanted to bring·him. I thought it might, just possibly, make me happy—or happier—to bring Robert with me this weekend. It seemed possible. Do you think I shouldn't have?"

"No," said Marian. "I'm sorry. I don't mean that. I don't know what I mean. I mean, I don't know what I mean in any well-thought-out way. I'm just . . . I'm fumbling." She paused for a moment, and then continued. "It's just difficult for me. I know it's ten million times more difficult for you, and I don't want to make it more difficult for you, or trivialize your difficulty. But I'm not going to pretend that this isn't difficult for me. It *is* awkward. Not to acknowledge that would be faking. It would be dishonest."

Lyle threw the crumbs into the trash. He wiped his hands back and forth, but he didn't say anything. He sat at the table.

Marian looked at him. "And now I feel awful," she said. "Now I feel as if I shouldn't have said anything. But

I couldn't have not said anything, because I know you too well. We've been through too much. You're my best friend." She stood behind him and put her hands, tentatively, on his shoulders. "And I love you too much," she said.

She stood like that, for a long moment, in the hot kitchen. Lyle had covered his eyes with one hand, even though she could not see him. She could only see the top of his head, his scalp through the thinning hair. He appeared, from this angle, old and frighteningly vulnerable. The eggshell of his scalp. She wanted to kiss it or lay her cheek against it but she did neither of these things. She squeezed gently at his shoulders. "I love you too much," she repeated. He took his right hand away from his eyes and reached back and patted her hand, and then laced his fingers through hers. And they were like that—having said nothing more, not crying, just Lyle sitting and Marian standing behind him and their hands pressed together on Lyle's shoulder—when Robert returned with the vegetables from the garden.

9

Lyle was sitting in an Adirondack chair in the shade. Robert was lying on the grass near him, in the sun, reading—or leafing through—a magazine. John was in the garden.

The back door opened and Marian appeared on the steps. She had gone inside to put Roland down for his nap. She walked across the lawn toward her guests, clutching some things in her hands.

"Come sit with us," said Lyle.

"No," she said, displaying what she held: the paint set Lyle had brought for Roland, and a pad, and a tumbler full of water. "I'm going to paint awhile. I want to try to do a sketch of the house from down near the river."

"Do you want us to move?" asked Lyle.

"Of course not," said Marian. "I'll paint you in."

"Those aren't very good paints," said Lyle.

"Then they'll suit me," said Marian. "Are you enjoying the sun, Robert?"

"Yes," said Robert. "It's great."

"Good," she said. She dragged another chair down the

lawn a ways and positioned it facing toward the house. Her distance from Lyle and Robert suggested, rather than guaranteed, their privacy.

She began painting, and listened to them talk, although she could not make out what they were saying. But after a while they began to speak more loudly. "Take you, for instance," she heard Robert say to Lyle. "You look better now than you did at thirty."

"Am better-looking," corrected Lyle. "But how do you know? You didn't know me when I was thirty."

"Marian showed me a picture," said Robert. "Of you and Tony in Egypt."

"Oh," said Lyle, "did she?"

Marian glanced up and found that Lyle was looking over at her. He made a face. "How's the painting?" he called. Robert turned his head.

Marian looked at her painting. It was not a success: the colors in the tiny compact were all wrong. They were intense and synthetic, and her attempts to mix them on the wet paper to suggest the sun-stunned colors around her had only muddied them. "It's a mess," she said. And then, as if such a judgment precluded continuation, she ripped the thick damp page from the pad and crumpled it up. She tossed it onto the lawn between them, where it unfurled itself slightly.

"I wanted to see it," said Lyle.

"I'll do another," Marian said. "I'll do one of you two." She turned her chair and in doing so upset the water goblet. "That was careless," she said.

"I'll fill it up," said Robert. He stood and crossed the lawn.

She handed him the glass. "Thank you," she said. She expected him to walk up to the spigot beside the back stoop, but instead he walked toward the river. Of course, she thought, Robert's a stranger here: he doesn't know where the spigot is. She knew this did not make him inferior in any way but she had a strange urge to think so. Stop it, she told herself. She watched him squat on a rock at the river's edge, dip the glass, and return. The river water was much clearer than she had imagined it would be. It was clear a glass at a time; only all together, flowing, was it opaque.

"Now go lie down," she said, "and pretend I'm not here."

Robert resumed his position, but Lyle had stood up.

"Sit down," said Marian. "I want to paint you."

Lyle frowned at her, and shook his head, and she understood that he did not wish to be painted. Was he angry with her for showing Robert the photograph? If he was, it was silly. She had merely pointed out something on the wall of her house.

"I feel in desperate need of a nap," Lyle said, and began walking quickly up the lawn, as if his need were indeed desperate, and he might collapse before he reached his bed. Marian and Robert watched him enter the house.

"I don't know how he can be tired," said Robert. "We've just lay about all afternoon."

Lain about, Marian wanted to say, but instead she said, "Sometimes indolence can be exhausting." She got up and sat down in Lyle's vacant chair. She felt she should offer to paint Robert, but she didn't really want to. His back, which had appeared smooth and brown from a distance, was actually, she now realized, pitted with acne scars.

"I thought Lyle brought those for Roland," Robert said, nodding at the paints.

"Oh, he did," said Marian, "but Roland is a baby. Lyle is a loving, but impractical, godfather."

"Lyle said he wanted Roland to be an artist. That's why he bought the paints."

"If only it were that easy," said Marian. "Or rather, thank God it's not."

"What do you want him to be?"

Marian wanted Roland to be alive the next morning. She avoided the question by asking, "Do you like children?"

Robert flipped a few pages of the magazine. "Yes," he said. "I like their hands. And feet."

Marian found this answer unnerving. It was as if she had asked him what part of the chicken he preferred. She looked away for a moment, trying to think of an appropriate response. None came to mind. "How old are you?" she asked.

"Twenty-four," said Robert. He looked at her. "I was twenty-four in June. How old are you?"

"I'm forty," said Marian. She looked at her hands for a moment, as if they might belie her. Then she patted her palms against the broad arms of her chair. "Well," she said, "I better check on Roland."

"Of course," said Robert, but in a way that let Marian know he knew she wanted to be away from him.

I did just put Roland down, Marian thought: I can't leave now. "We're so happy you're here," she said. She folded her hands in her lap.

"So am I," said Robert.

"And we're happy to see you with Lyle," said Marian.

Robert did not respond.

"What are you doing this summer?" Marian tried. "Besides painting, I mean."

"I have a job. As a waiter, in an Indian restaurant."

"Oh," said Marian. "Are you Indian?"

"My father is Indian. He lives in Delhi."

"What does he do?"

"He's a counterfeiter," said Robert.

"Oh," said Marian. "What does he counterfeit?"

"Different things that will make a lot of money. Mostly jeans, and sneakers."

"And your mother?" asked Marian.

"She's dead," said Robert. "She died when I was young."

"That's very sad," said Marian. "I'm so sorry. Was she American?"

"Yes," said Robert. "She was."

"How long have you been living over here?"

"About ten years," said Robert.

"Do you go back? Do you see your father often?"

Robert thought for a moment, as if this question required contemplation. "No," he said. "I haven't seen him in a while. I don't think he likes how I've turned out."

"Oh," said Marian, "you mean that you're an artist?"

"No," said Robert. "I meant he doesn't like that I'm gay."

"What a shame," said Marian.

"Would you be happy if Roland was gay?"

"Happy? Well, yes, I suppose. If he was happy."

"But you wouldn't be happy first? You'd wait for him to be happy, and then be happy?"

"Actually, to tell you the truth," said Marian, "this isn't something I've given any thought to. Roland is barely a year old. It seems a bit premature."

"Of course," said Robert. And then, after a moment, he added, "I'm sorry."

"There's no need to apologize," said Marian. She thought: He's not a bad person. I just don't like him. A bee alit on the lip of her glass of river water, and they both observed it. She waved it away. "I better go check on him," she said. She stood up. She felt defeated. "We won't be eating until about eight, so if you get hungry before then please help yourself to anything you can find. There's loads of fruit in the kitchen."

"Thank you," said Robert.

Marian paused for a moment, as if there was something else to be said, and then walked up toward the house. As she entered the kitchen, she heard the piano. She walked into the library and stood at the door.

Lyle was slowly and quietly picking his way through

some Bach, peering closely at the music. He stopped and said, "I'm terribly out of practice."

"It sounded good to me," said Marian.

"I'm sorry about rushing in here like that," said Lyle. "I just—" He shrugged. "I don't know." He played a few more notes, and then looked up. "Where's Robert?"

"He's still outside," said Marian.

"Alone?" asked Lyle.

"Yes," said Marian. "I came in to check on Roland."

"I haven't heard him," said Lyle. "I've been playing very quietly."

"Oh, don't worry about waking him. He's a good sleeper."

"Can we play something together, then?"

Marian smiled. "O.K.," she said. "Get up, and let's see what we have. I think it's all still in here."

Lyle stood up and she opened the bench and looked through the music. "What about the Hungarian Dances?" she asked.

"I'll murder it," said Lyle, "but let's give it a try."

They sat together on the bench, and Marian put the music on the stand. "We actually had this mastered," she said. "Remember?"

"Yes, but that was years ago."

"Only two," she said. "Let's see how much we've forgotten."

"Let me just look at it for a second," said Lyle. "I don't have my glasses, remember. That will be my excuse."

"Ready?" asked Marian, after a moment.

"Yes," said Lyle, "I suppose. Let's take it slowly."

Marian placed her hands on the keys beside Lyle's. She nodded her head, and they began to play. They did not do badly, and got quite far before Marian suddenly stopped. "Wait a second," she said. She listened. "I think that's Roland. Do you hear him?"

Lyle listened. "No," he said.

Marian stood up. "I'd better check. Come up with me."

He followed her upstairs and down the hall. Roland stood in his crib, but he wasn't crying. He was staring straight ahead of him, with a quizzical expression on his face.

"There you are," said Marian. "Look who's come to see you. Uncle Lyle." She picked him up.

"It looks like he could climb right out of there," said Lyle.

"He hasn't tried it yet," said Marian. "But I don't think it will be long. Are you stinky, darling? Yes, I think you are. Does Uncle Lyle want to change your diaper? Or should Mommy?"

"There are limits to Uncle Lyle's devotion," said Lyle.

Marian laughed, and kissed Roland's damp temple. "He's a bit warm," she said to Lyle. "Would you take that facecloth and run it under some cool water? I'll change him."

"Yes," said Lyle. He took the facecloth across the hall into the bathroom. It was a baby-sized facecloth, with yellow ducks, no bigger than his hand. He ran it under the tap and wrung it out, then moistened it again. Tony had worn diapers, his last days, in this house. Lyle had thought that changing Tony's diapers would be like changing a baby's diapers, but it had not been. It had been like changing a grown man's diapers. It might have been better if Tony's illness had made him a baby but it had not. He had never stopped being himself. Lyle realized he was pressing the damp cloth to his own face. He rinsed it out again and crossed the hall. Marian was sitting in the rocking chair nursing Roland. "Here," he said, handing her the cloth.

"Thanks," she said. She took the cloth and held it. "Sit down," she said, nodding at an easy chair covered with neat piles of laundry. "You can put that stuff on the dresser."

Lyle moved the folded clothes and sat in the chair. They were silent a moment, listening to the clutch and unclutch of Roland's mouth, and then Marian said, "So. What's going on?"

"What do you mean?" asked Lyle.

"The other day, on the phone, you said you had lots to tell me. I suppose now you were referring to Robert." She smoothed Roland's fine hair against his scalp with the cloth.

"Yes," said Lyle. "I suppose I was."

"So tell me about it. You met him at Skowhegan?"

"Yes," said Lyle. "But only briefly. Then he drove me down to the airport, and we got a chance to talk."

"And?"

"I found him interesting, and sweet. Most of the kids there were awful, so ambitious and confident and stupid and so totally unwilling to listen to anything. But Robert's different. He called me when he got back to New York, and I decided to offer him the use of Tony's study as a studio."

"Is he good?" asked Marian.

"I don't know," said Lyle. "It was more the idea of it, originally, that appealed to me: having somebody young and creative use the space. Don't you think Tony would have liked that?"

Marian shrugged. Tony had never seemed particularly interested in encouraging young artists. "Yes, I suppose," she said.

"I haven't seen his work. I have to admit I'm a bit scared about it now—what if it's awful? But I have a feeling it won't be. He says he paints 'contemporary landscapes.' "

"What? Gas stations and parking lots?"

"I don't know. I'll find out soon enough, I suppose. But I don't really care. It is the idea that counts. It seemed a relatively small thing for me, and it was such a big deal for him: to have a studio."

"But how did it get—well, romantic?"

"Romantic?"

"Well, isn't it? Or is it purely sexual?"

"No," said Lyle. "I suppose it's romantic. Whatever that means. And, much to my amazement, it's sexual, too. I don't know. You can't really explain these things, can you? They just happen."

"Yes, but you can try," said Marian: "It's important to understand why, don't you think? I mean, obviously there are reasons. What is it about him that you find so attractive?"

"What, you don't like him?"

"No," said Marian, "of course not. I mean, I don't

really know him yet. He seems very sweet. I'm just curious to know what attracted him to you."

"Well, to be perfectly honest and superficial, his looks. That always seems important at the beginning, doesn't it? I think he's very beautiful. And for some strange reason I don't understand, he seems to find me attractive. I like that."

"Of course he finds you attractive," said Marian. "You are."

"Well, it's not something I often feel," said Lyle.

"Then it's good, that he makes you feel it," said Marian.

"He's also—I don't know how to put this, really. I'm just figuring it out myself, I think. But he's open, somehow—I suppose because he's young—but I feel he hasn't made all his decisions yet, he isn't stuck thinking any one thing. He listens to people; he really listens."

"So you like him because he's malleable?"

"I suppose that's what I'm saying. But it's not so much that I'm interested in shaping him, or changing him. And he has a mind of his own. It's more how it makes me feel. He makes me think about what I do and say in a way I'd thought I'd stopped, or at least can't remember, doing."

"Hmm," said Marian. "That's an interesting thing about meeting new people: one sees oneself differently."

"Yes," said Lyle. "And I was feeling very stuck with how I was. Who I was. It's nice to know that even now one can change. At this late date."

"You aren't that old," said Marian.

"I've felt old, though," said Lyle.

"Well, don't change too much," said Marian. "I'm very fond of you as you are."

"Don't worry," said Lyle. "In fact, I don't even like to think about this all very much. I'd rather just let it happen. But I did want you to meet him. That's why I brought him."

"Well, I'm glad you did. It's not what I—well it was a surprise, as I'm sure you know. But a wonderful one. I'm very happy for you."

"Are you?" said Lyle. "Do you like him? I was worried that—"

"That what?"

"I don't know. I thought you might disapprove."

"Why? What is there to disapprove of?"

"I don't know," said Lyle. "It's just that it's all happened so quickly, and I don't quite feel right about it yet. Sometimes I still can't quite believe it. Basically, I don't know what I'm doing. All I know is that I'm happier than I've been in ages. Especially, now, being here, and talking to you about it."

Roland had fallen asleep. Marian stroked his cheek with the back of her fingers. They were silent a moment, and then Lyle said, "It's wonderful to see you. And to be here, and have a talk like this. I can't tell you how good it feels."

"I've missed you," she said.

"How are things with you?"

"Fine," she said.

"You haven't been depressed?"

"No," she said. "God, no. I don't—" She rocked for a moment. "That seems very long ago, although I know it isn't. I have a different life now. I really do. And it seems like the right one: now and here. Just not being in New York—you can't imagine what a difference that makes. How much simpler each day is. It's an awful thing to leave New York, because you feel that you'll cease to matter, to count. In a way it's like you're leaving the world. But you aren't at all. The world here is fine with me. And having Roland—well, that changes everything. Do you know that I haven't taken a pill since I was pregnant with him? Not even an aspirin."

"That's wonderful," said Lyle.

"I don't mean to say that medication isn't wonderful. It certainly saved me. But it can only do so much. I think it's mostly about finding the life that's right for you. It seems such an obvious thing, but it isn't. At least it wasn't for me. So much of my life was wrong. It scares me to think of all those people out there, living the wrong lives. And you don't realize it until it's almost too late. Until it becomes too horrible to bear."

"I'm so glad things are going well for you," said Lyle.

"And what about you?" asked Marian. "What about your work? Have you started a new book?"

"No. I have articles and I'm doing a lot of panels and lectures. Did I tell you I got a speaking agent?"

"No," said Marian. "Really?"

"Yes. He's the man Sigrid uses. It's amazing how many calls I get. Or got—it's slowing down, a bit, now. But next fall I'm traveling someplace almost every week."

"Goodness," said Marian. "You've become quite the star."

"Oh, you know how these things work. It won't last. But I figured I might as well exploit myself while I can."

"That's wonderful," said Marian. "I'm so happy for you. It's too bad that . . . Tony would have been so happy, too. To see you acclaimed. He would have been proud."

"Yes," said Lyle. "I know."

Marian looked down at Roland. "It's strange to have a child," she said. "It keeps surprising me. Sometimes I think that when Roland learns to talk he'll tell me everything. Everything he's thinking. That I will always know him entirely, as I feel I do now." She rocked for a moment. "I know it won't happen like that, but I think it." She looked up at Lyle and smiled. "But I guess we never know anyone like that, do we? Entirely?"

"No," said Lyle. "I guess not."

They sat for a moment. The day had plateaued into an hour or two of shimmering stillness, poised for its descent toward evening.

"I think I might take a nap, after all," Lyle said.

"It feels very sleepy, doesn't it?" Marian said.

Lyle stood up. He went over and kissed Marian, and touched Roland on his head. His hair was still damp from where it had been pushed back by the cloth. "Can we try the Dances again, later?"

"Yes," said Marian. "Now go have a nice nap."

10

The day was at its hot, still center, that hour or two on a midsummer afternoon when the sun seems to have found a niche in the sky it has no intention of ever abandoning. Lyle sat reading in a canvas sling-back chair on the dock. Tony was listlessly treading water around the dock's edges. He filled his cupped hands with water and poured it over Lyle's feet.

"Stop," said Lyle. "It's cold." He shook his feet, but he didn't look up from his book.

"I thought it would feel good," said Tony. "You looked hot."

Lyle continued reading.

"You have ugly feet," said Tony.

Lyle did not reply.

"I think feet in general are pretty ugly, but your feet are especially ugly."

"No they're not," said Lyle.

"If you look at them closely, they are," said Tony.

"Then don't look at them closely," said Lyle.

"Maybe if you look at anything closely enough it gets ugly," said Tony.

"That's not true," said Lyle.

"I guess ugly things get more ugly and beautiful things get more beautiful. But I bet some ugly things get beautiful and vice versa. What ugly things get beautiful the more you look at them?"

"I don't know," said Lyle. He looked up. "Insects, perhaps."

"Yes," said Tony, "exactly: insects. Actually, I like your feet. They're genuine. They're kind of Old World, and biblical." He kissed the bridge of Lyle's foot and then pushed himself back from the dock. "What are you reading?" he asked.

"Sigrid's new book," said Lyle.

"Is it good?" asked Tony.

"Not bad," said Lyle, "for Sigrid."

"What's it about?"

"The apocalypse. And art."

"Which apocalypse?"

"What do you mean, which apocalypse? There hasn't been an apocalypse yet. It's coming." Lyle put the book down and stretched out his feet. "Do that again, what you did. It felt good."

"Why don't you come in?"

"I will," said Lyle, "in a minute. But cool my feet."

"You're spoiled," said Tony, but he complied. "I want

to write a book," he said, as he watched the water spread out in a shadow around Lyle's feet.

"I'm always encouraging you to write a book," said Lyle.

"Not always," said Tony.

"Sometimes, then. What book do you want to write?"

"You say that as if it already exists, and it's just a matter of writing it," said Tony.

"That's how it should be with books. What would it be about?"

"It would be a travel book: a guide to a foreign country."

"What country?"

"An imaginary country." Tony placed his forearms on the edge of the deck and rested the side of his face on them. "I'd make it up. I'd make the whole country up, everything. All the cities and towns and restaurants and hotels and museums and cathedrals. Or maybe not cathedrals. I don't think they'd be cathedrals in this country. They'd be more of something else, something more fun, like nightclubs. Or spas. I'd draw all the maps, of each county and city, every street, maps of the subway systems even. Lots of maps."

"That sounds like quite a project," said Lyle.

"It would always be the nineteenth century in this

country, I think. But with electricity and plumbing. But no cars. Trains and ships, but no cars."

"Humans are always sentimentally attached to the century that immediately precedes their own," said Lyle.

"Is that thought your own?"

"Of course," said Lyle. "All my thoughts are my own."

"They often don't sound like it," said Tony. "But don't you think there was something inherently nice about the nineteenth century?"

"No," said Lyle. "It's a century that appeals only to imperialists like you."

"I think I'm a royalist, not an imperialist. I suppose I'm both. I like order. That's why I'm glad I shall only live in one century. Even if it's the wrong one. It must be confusing when one's life bridges the centuries. Like Monet. My grandmother was born in 1900. I would like that: to grow old with the century. It was very neat."

Lyle had returned his attention to Sigrid's book.

"I thought you were going to swim," said Tony.

"I was," said Lyle. "I am."

"Swim now," said Tony.

"I don't swim on command," said Lyle. "Look: here comes Marian."

Marian was walking down the lawn toward them. She

and John were trying to get pregnant, and were making love according to a schedule posted on the refrigerator.

"Mission accomplished?" Tony called out as Marian stepped onto the dock.

"Well, I did my part," said Marian.

"Did John do his?" asked Tony.

"Yes," said Marian.

"I wonder if you feel it, when you become pregnant."

"I think it takes a while." Marian sat down on the edge of the dock, her sundress bunched up, her legs in the water.

"Do you make love differently when you're trying to get pregnant?" asked Tony.

"I don't know," said Marian. "I forget what it's like to make love and not try to get pregnant."

"You sound so heterosexual," said Tony. "Maybe you're trying too hard. Maybe if you forgot about it, it would happen. Like how you remember something only when you've stopped trying to remember it."

"I don't have time to forget about it," said Marian.

"I feel no desire to procreate," said Tony. "Would you like to have a child?" he asked Lyle.

"Yes," said Lyle. "Theoretically."

"You can't have a theoretical child," said Marian.

"I know," said Lyle. "But I like the idea of having a

child. I think I'd like a ward. But wards are rather scarce nowadays, aren't they?"

"It's the century," said Tony. "In my country there will be plenty of wards."

"What country?" asked Marian.

"I'm going to write a book about a perfect country where it's always the nineteenth century and where there are plenty of wards," said Tony. "With maps. And appendices."

"It's hot," said Marian. "I should have put on my bathing suit."

"You don't need it," said Tony. "I don't have mine."

"You never have yours."

Tony splashed her. "Take off your dress. Come in."

"You've got it wet now."

"Take it off."

Marian stood up and pulled her dress off over her head. She was naked beneath it. "How decadent we are," she said.

"How American of you to equate nudity with decadence," said Tony.

Marian dove into the water. She surfaced and said, "It's lovely."

"Are you supposed to swim so soon after?" asked Lyle.

"I've spent the last twenty minutes with my feet up in

the air," said Marian. "If it hasn't happened by now, forget it. And let's stop talking about it. It jinxes it, I'm sure. Do you want to swim up to the rock, Tony?"

"All right, but slowly. Are you coming, Lyle?"

"No," said Lyle. "I'm in no mood to exhaust myself. I'll stay here and watch you."

"Come," said Tony.

"No," said Lyle. "Wave to me when you get there."

11

Robert fell asleep on the lawn, his face pressed against the magazine he had been reading, so that when he awoke, he found the page blurred. Some of the ink had rubbed off—a smudged moist tattoo—onto his cheek. He noticed that Marian had left her paints and pad behind, and he couldn't resist doing a few sketches: one of an Adirondack chair and its sharp dark shadow on the green lawn, one of the table ensconced beneath the mulberry tree, and one of the pile of croquet balls and mallets. By then the water in the glass had turned a pearly gray, and he poured it onto the lawn.

He walked down to the edge of the river, squatted, and tested the water with his hands. It was cold. Somewhere beyond the bend of the river he could hear people laughing and splashing, and a dog barking. Then it was quiet and he could actually hear the flow of the water. He could hear John singing to himself beyond the hedge. And a rustling, high in the trees. After a few minutes he walked up to the house. He selected a peach from the bowl on the kitchen table and ate it. The juice ran down his hands and when he was finished eating the peach he sucked his fingers and then rinsed them beneath the faucet. It was very quiet in the house. He walked through the kitchen into the front hall and then into a cool shuttered room with a low beamed ceiling. A grand piano stood near the window. It was opened and there was some music on the stand. Bookshelves were built along every wall, and a traveling ladder was connected to them via a copper tube. There was a terra-cotta urn of what looked like sea glass in the empty fireplace. A round table stood before the fireplace with an enormous vase crowded with flowers at its center. Spread out around the vase were magazines and a few stacks of books—new books. There were five copies of Lyle's *Neo This, Neo That* in their own little pile. Robert opened one and glanced through it. It was inscribed: *To Granger and Derek with Love from Lyle*. He looked at the photograph of Lyle in the back: Lyle was standing against the stone wall of the house, a shadow of leaves across his face. The credit was Marian Richardson Kerr. Robert put the book down.

He looked at the photographs on the mantelpiece: there was one of John and Marian as a very beautiful bride and groom, one of John holding an ugly baby Robert assumed was Roland, one of an old lady sitting in an easy chair with two small dogs with jeweled collars poised alertly on her lap, and one of Lyle and Tony standing on a balcony, a city that looked like Paris spread out behind them. Robert took this picture down and studied it. Tony had his arm around Lyle and was looking directly at the camera; Lyle was looking a little bit up and away. Tony's bare wrist touched Lyle's neck, and the cigarette he held looked about to drop its cylinder of ash on Lyle's shoulder. Tony was very handsome. His beautiful face was muscular and intent, sculpted, and his gaze was direct but not confronting. It was seen as easily as it saw. Both Lyle and Tony were smiling. They looked happy. It was Paris, Robert noticed—a distant silhouette of the Eiffel Tower. He wondered if he would ever travel anywhere with Lyle. And then he reminded himself that was what he was doing. I am traveling with Lyle. I am here with Lyle. He put the picture carefully back on the mantel, trying to refit it to its pattern in the dust.

I am here with Lyle.

He climbed the back stairs and walked along the hall. He didn't realize he was headed in the wrong direction until he passed a room where Marian sat in a rocking chair before an open window nursing Roland. They were both asleep. Roland's mouth had slipped off Marian's nipple but he continued to pulse his lips. Marian's head lolled to one side and her mouth was open. Her face looked different to Robert: as if a veil of tension had been lifted, something you could not notice until it was gone. Robert watched for a moment and then turned around and walked, past the stairs, to the opposite end of the house.

When he turned into the hall of photographs he saw that the door to the yellow room was closed. It seemed closed in a way that discouraged one from opening or knocking on it: it was the only door closed on a long hall of many doors. Trapezoids of sunlight fell through the open doors onto the wooden floor of the hall. Robert stood for a moment, wondering what to do. He looked at the wall of photographs beside him and noticed a strange thing: a space, in the middle of the wall, where a photograph had been removed. He knew it was the photograph of Lyle and Tony in Egypt because beside it was the photograph of Lyle dressed as a pirate. Robert looked at the empty space.

He walked down the hall and opened the door of the yellow room. The afternoon light poured, like weak honey-eyed tea, through the paper shades. He could hear an insect whirring and whining, batting itself against a screen. Lyle was sleeping naked, face-down, on the bed. His limbs were splayed in a way that suggested he had been dropped from the sky.

Robert sat on the bed. He looked at Lyle. It was odd how Lyle's body—large, hairy, white—could flicker in and out of beauty. He had been attracted to Lyle when he first saw him at Skowhegan, in an abstract, unacknowledged way. And the more he got to know Lyle, the more beautiful Lyle's body seemed to him: this vessel for the contents that were Lyle. Now, stilled on the bed, shaking quietly with breath, it seemed like one of those sculptures smoothed from rock that insist on being touched. Lyle's back was sweating. Robert resisted the urge to bend over and lick it. He was scared of how sexy he found Lyle, afraid of alienating Lyle with his desire. He found almost everything about Lyle sexy: his body, his mind, his talk, the way he climbed stairs, the way his fingers gripped a fork, blushing with tension, the way he smelled and tasted, the impossibly soft way his back and neck and shoulders congregated, the spot there, the crux of him, naked and lickable.

Robert traced the corrugated route of Lyle's spine down toward the tight valley of his buttocks. This motion, though intended to, did not rouse Lyle. And then Robert realized that Lyle was awake, and pretending to sleep. The skin across his shoulders gave him away—it was suddenly elastic with tension. It was not the skin of a sleeper. Robert removed his hand and got up. He stood beside the bed for a moment, looking down at Lyle, who continued to feign sleep. Neither of them spoke. And then Robert saw the photograph of Lyle and Tony and the camel and the pyramids on the table beside the bed.

He left the room. He went outside and stood in the front yard for a moment, and then walked up the long dirt driveway. The paved road it adjoined was surprisingly heavily traveled. The cars sped by noisily, blowing up hot storms of wind and dust as they passed. Robert began to walk along the side of the road, on the shoulder of a gulch. The gulch was full of stagnant water and soda cans; on its other side was a field of tall corn. Robert jumped across the ditch and walked between two rows of corn, far enough into the field so that he could not see the traffic. He sat on the ground and pulled his knees up against his chest and rested his forehead on them. It felt cool and peaceful in the corn. He could see the ground between his legs and watched some ants drag a piece of corn husk across his field of vision. Maybe I was wrong, he thought: maybe Lyle really was sleeping. I should have woken him up. I should have spoken to him. I shouldn't have just left. I love Lyle, he thought.

He got up and retraced his steps, but instead of going back along the driveway, he veered off into the woods. He thought that would be the quickest way to get back to Lyle.

After Robert left, Lyle lay on the bed for a while. For a moment after he awoke he had thought the hand on his back was Tony's. And as quickly as he thought that—it wasn't even as deliberate as thinking: the hand, for an instant, was Tony's—he realized it was Robert's hand. Tony is dead, he told himself. It was strange that the most momentous event of his life—the death of his lover— seemed sometimes to be so tentatively attached to his consciousness. He often awoke to, or dreamed of, a world where Tony was alive. Not a world in which Tony had come back to life, but a world in which Tony existed, as he had existed, where his existence was more often tolerated than appreciated. For Tony and Lyle had not always loved one another very well, and this fact made Lyle's mourning all the more complicated. His sadness at losing Tony was ornamented with guilt.

Lyle sat up. I need a swim, he thought. I'll go find Robert and we'll have a swim. He could imagine the cold clean water of the river around him. He called Robert's name, softly, as if he might be waiting just outside the door. But of course there was no answer. Lyle put on his bathing suit and a T-shirt and a pair of sandals and went downstairs. He walked through the house and saw no one. He went out the back door and down the lawn, through a chink in the hedge, and stopped beside the garden. John was doing something fierce with a hoe: thrusting it into the ground, wriggling it, and removing it. Lyle stood outside the gate for a moment, watching John, and then he said, "Have you seen Robert?"

John poked the hoe into the ground and turned around. He wiped his brow with the back of his hand. "No," he said. "Are you going for a swim?"

"Yes," said Lyle. "But I was looking for Robert."

"Where's Marian?"

"I don't know. She's disappeared, too."

"I doubt they've run off together," said John. He wiggled the hoe, and then reinserted it, more firmly, into the earth. "Well, I'm through gardening. Let's swim. Robert will find us, I'm sure." He took off his T-shirt and wiped the sweat from his body with it and then carefully hung it over the garden fence, to air in the sun. "Let's go," he said to Lyle.

They began to walk down toward the river. "I like Robert," said John. "He seems awfully nice."

"Yes," said Lyle. "He is."

Robert's watercolor sketches lay on the arm of an Adirondack chair. They paused to look at them.

"Who did those?" asked John.

"Marian," said Lyle. "She was going to paint Robert and me, but I went inside. They're awfully good." He picked up the one of the croquet apparatus and looked at it more closely. "They shouldn't be here in the sun," he said. He put the sketches down on the lawn in the chair's shadow. "They're really very nice. Remind me to bring them into the house."

"O.K.," said John.

They reached the bank of the river and walked to the end of the dock, carefully avoiding the planks that had lost their grips. They loitered there, as if they had intended to walk across the river and were surprised to find the dock extended only this far.

John knelt and dangled his fingers in the water. "What do you think of Roland?" he asked.

"Roland? What do you mean?"

"Marian's worried about him. She thinks—I don't know, that he's slow. That maybe there's something wrong with him, developmentally."

"I'm hardly the person to consult," said Lyle.

"I know," said John. "I just wondered how he struck you."

"He seemed normal enough to me. He sleeps a lot."

"All babies sleep a lot."

"Well, then, he seems very normal. When is he supposed to start walking?"

"Anytime about now. He doesn't really crawl yet. And he's not very responsive."

"What does the doctor say?"

"That he has low scores in certain areas but we shouldn't worry about it. That low means low, not abnormal."

"Then you shouldn't worry."

"Marian does. She's—I don't know. She won't let herself be reassured. If you think of it, say something to her. I think if you said something it would mean a lot to her."

"Like what?"

John shrugged. He flicked the water from his fingers into the river, and stood up. "I don't know. Just something reassuring. I mean, you haven't seen Roland since he was tiny. Surely he's changed in some ways."

Things must be very bad, Lyle thought, for John to ask me to do that.

John bent over and unlaced his sneakers and took off his shorts and underwear. He stood for a moment, naked, his toes curled around the edge of the final plank. From behind he looked very much like Tony. From behind he almost could have been Tony. John stood still for a moment, as if he knew that Lyle was studying him, and then he dove, neatly, into the river. He didn't resurface until the stain of his entrance had been absorbed. He had swum out very far. John motioned for Lyle to join him. Lyle considered for a moment shedding his bathing suit, but did not. His dive was less exact.

Robert got lost in the woods and found himself on the bank of the river. Lyle and John were swimming out in the middle. Or not swimming—treading water, being slowly carried downstream with the current. Robert stood for a moment, watching them, and then took off his clothes and waded into the river. The mud was slimy and unpleasant beneath his feet. He held his arms up in the air and felt the chill ascend his body. He dove into the water with enough noise and force so that when he surfaced both John and Lyle were looking toward him. He tried to wave at them while he swam but the movement was awkward. He was a mediocre swimmer and the distance to them was greater than he had thought. He arrived at their side breathless.

"There you are," said Lyle. "I was wondering where you were."

"I went for a walk," Robert said, between gasps.

They were all three silent for a moment. Robert had the feeling he had interrupted something. "I think I'll swim to that rock," he said.

"You'd better get your breath back first," said John.

"I'm fine," said Robert. "It's just the cold water that makes me pant." He began swimming upstream. When he turned around, John and Lyle were swimming toward the house. Robert floated on his back and watched them get out of the water and stand on the dock. They waved at him to return, but he purposefully misinterpreted their gesture and waved back. He waited until they were walking up the lawn before he began slowly swimming back to where he had left his clothes. The sun had sunk behind the trees, and the water, luminous moments ago, was now dark.

12

It was a large rock—a boulder—on a kind of shoal about a quarter of a mile upstream. Marian reached it first, drew herself up onto it, and lay down in the sun. She sat up when she heard Tony approach. "Come on, come on," she said.

"It amazes me that I can still do this," he said, as he hoisted himself beside her. "If I actually exercised regularly, think what a hunk I would be." He lay beside her, face-down in the hot sun, panting. "Why are you in such good shape?" he asked.

"I'm not, really. But swimming is easy for me, for some reason. I've always been a good swimmer. Look: wave to Lyle. He's waving."

"Oh, let him wave," said Tony. "He needs the exercise."

Marian waved and then lay back down. "It's worth it, isn't it? To swim here. To feel like this."

"Like what?" asked Tony.

"Exhausted," said Marian. "But happy. And warm, after being cold. I like to be exhausted. I wish I were always exhausted like this. I could fall asleep."

"It's all the sex you've been having," said Tony.

"Uhhmm," said Marian. She swatted a fly that had landed on her stomach.

"Don't fall asleep," said Tony. "Talk to me."

"What about?" asked Marian.

"I don't know. About all the sex you've been having. Is John a good lover?"

"Yes," said Marian. "But you shouldn't ask questions like that."

"Why not?"

"Because what if he weren't? Besides, it's none of your business, really."

"Why do you think people are so reluctant to talk about sex?" asked Tony.

"I suppose because it's private," said Marian. "It's intimate. People like to keep it between themselves." She smiled a little, her eyes closed, her face angled toward the sun.

"I used to have a crush on John," said Tony. "When I was about ten, and he was a teenager. My butch half-brother teenager from America. I was obsessed with him. It's how I realized I was gay."

"I trust you've gotten over it," said Marian.

"Yes," said Tony. "It was just a phase. He doesn't seem sexy to me anymore."

"He's sexy to me," said Marian. "What about Lyle? Is he a good lover?"

Tony turned over and looked toward the dock. Lyle had draped Marian's sundress over his head to shield him from the sun. "I don't think sex is a high priority with Lyle," he said.

"It is with you?" asked Marian.

"Yes," said Tony. "As a matter of fact, I like sex."

"Lyle doesn't?"

"Not as much as me."

"Is that a problem?" asked Marian.

"Not really," said Tony.

"Are you faithful?"

"How do you mean?" asked Tony.

"You know how I mean. Are you monogamous?"

"No," said Tony. "When I travel, sometimes, I have . . . liaisons."

"Does Lyle know that?"

"Yes," said Tony, "although we don't really discuss it."

"Then how does he know?"

"Because he knows." Tony lay back down, this time face-up.

"Do you think he sees other men?"

"Lyle?" said Tony. "No."

"But you're not sure?" asked Marian.

"No," said Tony. "Why? Do you know differently?"

"No," said Marian. "Not that I'd tell you if I did."

"We're happy together," Tony said. "That's the important part."

"Yes," said Marian. "I agree."

They were quiet a moment and then Marian said, "What's it like to have liaisons?"

"What do you mean?"

"I mean, what's it like? How does it make you feel?"

"I don't know," said Tony. "I only do it sometimes. If I happen to meet someone I'm particularly attracted to, who seems interested."

"That doesn't happen often?" asked Marian.

"Often enough."

"Do you see such a person more than once?"

"Not usually. Sometimes."

"Do you ever think you might fall in love with one of them? Or they with you?"

"No," said Tony.

"But there's nothing to stop love from occurring, is there?"

"I suppose not," said Tony. "But it doesn't."

"You're careful, aren't you? When you have these liaisons?"

"What do you mean?"

"You know what I mean," said Marian. "Are you safe?"

"Yes," said Tony.

"Good," said Marian. "I worry about you."

Tony was silent a moment, and then said, "Although it's a little too late for it to matter."

"What?" asked Marian. "For what to matter?"

"I'm HIV positive," said Tony.

Marian sat up. Tony lay still, his eyes closed.

"I'm sorry," said Marian.

Tony said nothing.

"How long have you known?"

"A while," said Tony. "About four years."

"Four years! Why haven't you told me?"

"I had decided not to tell anyone, until I thought it mattered. Except Lyle, of course."

"I'm glad you told me. I'm just— I'm shocked. And sad. Although I know—I mean, well, think of Granger. He's been HIV positive for years and years and he's the healthiest person I know."

"Yes," said Tony. "Granger's very healthy. Like an ox. Or is it a horse?"

"Are you healthy?" asked Marian.

"As healthy as I ever was," said Tony. "Let's drop it for now, though. I don't know why I brought it up. I don't like to dwell on it, especially on a day like today." He sat up.

"O.K.," said Marian. "Should we go back? Are you ready?"

"I think I'll stay out here awhile," said Tony. "Tell Lyle to come get me in the punt. I doubt he'll swim out."

"All right," said Marian. "Should I send a beer with him?"

"That would be great," said Tony. "I'd love a beer."

"Is there anything else you want?" asked Marian.

"No," said Tony. "Just Lyle and a beer."

Marian stood up. For a moment she didn't move. She was looking toward the dock, and then she looked down at Tony. It appeared to him that she was crying. He put his hand up to shield his eyes, but as he did Marian turned and dove into the water. A little of her splash flung itself back onto his hot skin.

Marian drew herself up onto the dock and said to Lyle, "Tony wants you to go get him in the boat."

"If he swam out there, he can swim back," said Lyle.

"No," said Marian. She pulled her dress off Lyle's head and slid it over her own. "Go," she said. "Get the boat. It's in the shed. I'm going up to get him a beer. You can bring it out to him."

"What's this all about?" asked Lyle. "Since when do we cater to Tony?"

Marian looked as if she might hit him. "Since now," she said. "Go."

13

"How was your swim?" Lyle asked, as Robert strode up the lawn. He was sitting in an Adirondack chair carefully placed on the one small ragged patch of sun that remained.

"Good," said Robert.

"I didn't know you were such a swimmer. Is that how you keep so fit?"

Robert didn't know what to say. He was not a swimmer. It had been a miserable swim. He felt for a moment like crying.

"Careful," said Lyle. "Don't drip on Marian's paintings."

Robert looked down at the sketches that were spread on the lawn. They were good, he realized. "They're mine," he said.

"Are they?" said Lyle. "I should have known. I thought they were awfully good for Marian."

"Marian told you she did them?"

Lyle laughed. "No. I just assumed she did, since she had the paints. May I have one?"

"Do you want one?" asked Robert.

"I don't ask for things I don't want," said Lyle.

"Which one?"

Lyle pointed, with his toe, to the painting of the chair. Then he reached up and touched one of Robert's nipples, which was shriveled with cold. Robert shivered. "Sit down," Lyle said. "You're freezing. I brought a towel out for you. Let me warm you up." He patted his lap.

Robert hesitated. He was not sure he wanted to sit on Lyle's lap. But Lyle reached up and pulled him down, and then gathered Robert in his arms, wrapping him in a towel that felt as thick as a blanket. He held him close. "I'm sorry," Lyle said, "about before. I was awake."

"I know," said Robert. His teeth were chattering, from cold but also from some sense of nervousness.

"I was just a little . . . disoriented," said Lyle. "But I should have said something. I shouldn't have pretended to be sleeping. And about the picture. The photograph. I was just looking at it, you know, and . . . I meant to put it back up. But I fell asleep. I'm sorry."

"It's O.K.," said Robert.

"Is it?" asked Lyle. "Are you?"

"Am I what?"

"O.K."

"Yes," said Robert. "Now."

"Good," said Lyle. "That's what I want. Did you go for a walk?"

"Just a little."

"Where?" Lyle kissed Robert's bare back.

"Just down the road. There's a cornfield out there."

"Maybe we'll have some corn for dinner. I'd love some corn. Do you like corn?"

"Yes," said Robert.

"This is my favorite time of day," said Lyle. "Early evening, midsummer. The world seems very perfect, doesn't it?"

"How can it be very perfect?" asked Robert. "It's either perfect or not."

"No," said Lyle. "There are many gradations of perfection. God was generous in that way."

"Do you believe in God?" asked Robert.

"Intermittently," said Lyle.

"I don't," said Robert. "And I think perfection is absolute."

"You sound like me," said Lyle. He kissed him again, and then ungently bit the place he had kissed. "Are you warm yet?" he asked.

"No," said Robert. "Almost."

Lyle rubbed Robert's arms and then held him again, tighter. Very tightly. He moved his face so that he could reach his tongue into Robert's ear, adjusted their positions so that his erection pressed more comfortably against Robert's ass, and said, "Tell me when you're nice and warm."

Upstairs, in the bedroom, Robert shut the door. Lyle sat on the bed. Robert came over and knelt on the floor, placing his face on Lyle's lap, on his damp bathing suit. It smelled of the river, and, more faintly, of Lyle. He could see Lyle's hand poised on the peony-patterned bedspread. He picked it up and placed it on top of his own head. Lyle held it still for a moment, and then began to sift his fingers through Robert's damp hair. "Wait," Lyle said, standing up. He peeled off his bathing suit and tossed it on the floor. He watched Robert step out of his shorts and then they both lay down, cool and naked, on the bed.

They lay like that for a moment, parallel, staring up at the ceiling, floating in the infused light of the yellow room, and then they turned toward one another.

14

"Listen," said Marian, "can I stick him in with you?" She stood in the bathroom door, holding Roland. John was lying in the bathtub, reading the newspaper.

"Why?" he asked.

"I want to go for a walk. I won't be long." She began to undress Roland.

"Where are you going?"

"Just out. For a walk."

"What's wrong?" asked John.

"Nothing's wrong. I just feel like getting away for a bit. By myself."

"Are you all right?"

"Of course I'm all right. I'm fine. I'm just going for a walk."

"What are Lyle and Robert doing?"

"Resting, I think. They're behind closed doors."

"What time is it?"

"About 5:30. I told them we'd have a cocktail about seven. Move your legs." She picked up the denuded Roland and lowered him into the bath. "Here," she said to John. "Give me the newspaper."

John handed her the paper. "I was about to get out," he said.

"No you weren't," said Marian. "But get out if you want. I won't be long. And will you keep an eye on him this time?"

"What do you mean?" asked John.

"I mean this morning. When I came back from the station he was playing with a croquet wicket. I was furious."

"I was watching him," said John.

"No," said Marian. "You weren't. If you were watching him properly he wouldn't have been playing with the wickets."

"I was watching him. I had my eye on him. You can't watch him every second."

"Yes," said Marian, "you can."

"What's made you so ferocious?" asked John.

"Nothing," said Marian. "I'm not ferocious. That's an awful thing to call someone. Just watch him for me, will you?"

"Of course," said John.

Marian walked out the front of the house and partway up the driveway and then entered the woods. They were pleasantly moist. There was a subtle mingling of scents of decay and dryness, and the sun fell to pieces through the dense canopy of leaves. She walked down to the stream and followed it until she came to the little log bridge where she had stood the morning—the moment perhaps—that Tony had died. The bridge was still intact, but the stream had changed. Its roar had been reduced to a patient flow. Marian knelt and interrupted it with her fingers. The water was cold and clear; it magnified the leaves and ferns pressed to the rocks beneath it. Some animals so small she couldn't tell if they were insects or fish swam lazily through it. She leaned down closer to the water. She no longer saw her reflection in it—she was so close her breath disturbed its surface. She thought: It's very difficult to memorialize the dead. To make a remembrance of them that is not an indulgence of your grief is almost impossible. And you will never have them again untainted by your sorrow, never think of them, or see them, with a clean flurry of feeling, but always with this grief, this sorrow, this selfish feeling of abandonment, which is more about you than about them. She hated feeling sorry for herself that Tony was dead.

When she had been in the hospital Tony was the only person she could really bear to see. She felt guilty with everyone else. With John, and her mother—with Lyle, even—she had felt guilty, as if she had to explain what had happened, explain her inability to live. But not with

Tony. He had spoken to her about God, although he had never mentioned God before and never did again after. He told her that she needed faith. A faith. Some kind of faith. Otherwise, it was too easy to let go of life. You had to make up a God that you could believe in and then believe in it. You had to believe that there was something present in your life that could save you. You did not necessarily need to know what it was but you had to feel that it existed. You had to find what delighted you about life and seize it. You could not let it go, or lose sight of it. You had to grow claws with which to grasp it.

That is what Tony had told her. And she had said, Yes, I know.

And can you do that? Tony had asked.

No, she had said. I understand you, but I can't. It's not like—I don't have the power to do that. I have no control. It's like I'm walking along a cliff. A high sheer cliff above the sea, like in a movie. The White Cliffs of Dover, for instance. And the cliff curves in and out. But I have to keep walking straight. I can't turn or adjust my route to suit the cliff. I have to keep walking straight. And sometimes I come very close to the edge. I come too near the edge. And there is nothing I can do.

There is nothing I can do.

A moth floated by, batting its chalky wings on the

water's surface, panicked. Marian leaned forward to rescue it, but the current was too fast. She sat back on the bridge and looked at her watch. It was getting late. The sunlight was fading, withdrawing in long, mote-filled shafts. It was time to go back. To go back and be herself. To be that person she was. To go back and be alive.

15

The nearest supermarket wasn't very super, but it had genuineness and intimacy, characteristics Laura appreciated. Even the shopping carts seemed from a different, better, era. Nina took one and entered the first aisle, which was produce.

"We'll stop at the farm stand on the way home," said Laura. "The produce here is pretty terrible."

Nina was palming an anemic tomato. "Yes," she said.

"But the meat is excellent," said Laura. "Are you going to use the grill?"

"Yes," said Nina. "We might as well."

"Then we should get some charcoal."

They turned the corner into the second aisle. Nina began to toss things in the cart that could, but Laura felt sure wouldn't, be used for dinner. She didn't make an issue of it. She'd buy whatever Nina wanted.

"It's nice to see you, finally," she said.

"It's too bad you're going out to dinner," said Nina.

"Yes," said Laura. "If I'd known you were coming . . ."

"What?"

"I told you. I'd have asked for you to be invited. But I really doubted you'd come this weekend. After not showing up for six weekends, it seemed foolish to believe you would."

"But you could have told them I might be coming, that there was a possibility."

"Actually, I thought of it. But I don't really think they're the kind of people you'd like."

"Why not?"

"Oh, they're very earnest, and American."

"What do you mean, they're American? You're American."

"Technically, I am. But I didn't mean nationalistically. I meant temperamentally."

Nina was rooting through the freezer of ice cream, a large open well, encrusted with smoking ice. "You sound like such a snob," she said.

"I never said I wasn't," said Laura. "Everyone's a snob. It's part of human nature."

"But not a very nice part," said Nina. She tossed a torpedo-shaped container of ice cream into the cart.

"I think you have a lot of gall cross-examining me about this," said Laura. "I came all the way to New York to be near you this summer, but have you spent any time with me? No. So forgive me if I spend an evening in the company of strangers."

"You didn't come to New York to be near me," Nina said, calmly. She continued down the aisle.

"Oh?" said Laura, aware that she was raising her voice. "Didn't I? Then what did I come all this way for?"

"I don't know," said Nina. "To escape something. To get away from someone. But not to see me. Or maybe to see me, but not to be near me. Not to spend time with me."

"You're ridiculous," said Laura. "That's precisely what I came here for."

"So now I'm here," said Nina. "And you're going out to dinner."

"Yes," said Laura. "I'm going out to dinner. For four hours. Imagine! Four hours. It's criminal."

Nina turned the cart around the corner and studied

the tins of coffee. "Let's not talk about this anymore," she said. She took two tins—one caffeinated, one decaffeinated—off the shelf and put them in the cart. "I didn't mean to get you all upset."

"I'm not upset," said Laura. "I just don't understand the point of your coming up here if you're just going to antagonize me."

"I didn't mean to be antagonistic," said Nina. "I meant to be honest."

"Well, spare me your honesty," said Laura.

Nina looked at her mother. "Fine," she said. "I will."

16

Tony was shaving. A juice glass filled with white wine sat on the ledge of the bathroom sink, refracting the evening light. Lyle lay reading on the sofa.

"I might go back into the city tonight," Tony said.

Lyle put down his book but did not answer.

"Not till late," said Tony. "On the 9:45. If I go."

"To see someone?" asked Lyle.

"No," said Tony.

"Then can I come with you?"

"Don't you want to stay here?"

"Yes," said Lyle. "Of course I do. But not if you're not."

"Why not?" asked Tony.

"Why are you going back?" asked Lyle.

"I didn't say I was. I said might."

"Why might you go back?"

Tony pulled the razor along his throat. He shaved twice a day. He liked how it felt to shave: to scrape away a layer, to rejuvenate himself. He always felt younger after he shaved. "Actually," he said, "to tell you the truth, I might see someone. It depends if he's left a message."

Lyle picked up his book and pretended to read for a moment, but he had lost his ability to follow the text from one line to the next. He could read across the line, but at the end it was like falling off a cliff. Without lowering the book, he said, "Why would you tell me that? That you might be going back to meet someone, when it isn't even definite? Why would you do that?"

"To prepare you," said Tony. "So I don't just run off." He held his razor beneath the faucet. A trail of blood spiraled, turning less and less red, down the drain. "Last time I left without telling you, you were angry."

"Yes," said Lyle. "I was. And I am now."

"I'm sorry," said Tony. "Anyway, he probably won't call. I think I'm too old for him."

"I don't understand you," said Lyle. "Why would you want to leave here, in the middle of the most beautiful weekend, to go back to the city to have sex with a relative stranger?"

Tony patted his shaved face with a towel, and took a sip of the wine. "We've talked about this," he said. "I don't know why I want what I want." He came and sat beside Lyle on the sofa. "Don't be angry," he said. "You know it's just. . . . You know it doesn't matter to me."

"But it matters to me," said Lyle.

"I'm sorry about that," said Tony. "Truly, I am. You know I am." He offered Lyle the wine.

Lyle declined by shaking his head. "You should get dressed," he said. "We should go downstairs. And you're bleeding," he said. "Beneath your chin."

"Shit," Tony said. He got up and looked in the mirror, then held a piece of toilet paper against his chin. He stood looking out the window. He watched Marian walk about the lawn, lighting citronella candles. She wore a white dress and was barefoot. "I won't go," he said. "I'm sorry. I won't even call the machine."

"Go if you want," said Lyle. "Don't do me any favors."

Tony turned away from the window. Lyle appeared to be reading. "I don't do this to hurt you," he said.

"I know," said Lyle. "But it does. You do."

"Sometimes . . . I mean, we've talked about this, Lyle. We have. I thought we had an understanding. I want to enjoy my life while I still can. And I enjoy, sometimes, having sex with other men. I'm not ashamed of it and I don't think I should be. It's about my body, and theirs. It isn't about my mind or how I feel for you. You said you understood."

"I do," said Lyle. "I just don't want to hear about it. That's all."

"But then you get angry if I disappear, or if I'm dishonest. You can't have it both ways."

Lyle thought: I don't want it both ways. I don't want it at all. After a moment he said, "How's your chin?"

Tony removed the paper and looked in the mirror. "It's stopped," he said. "I think it's fine."

17

Robert showered—as well as he could in the bathtub—and dressed for dinner. He left Lyle shaving in the bathroom and walked down the hall. He opened the door to the back staircase, and heard Marian's voice.

"What do you think of him?" she was saying.

"He seems nice," said John. "Young."

"I don't like him," said Marian.

"Why not?"

"He's . . . there's something prickly about him."

"Well, it must be awkward for him. Coming here, and us being so close to Lyle. And having been so close to Tony."

"I understand that. I mean apart from that. There's just something about—I hate young people who are judgmental. Who observe you and judge you and think they know better. He's like that, I can tell."

"But you're judging him."

"Well, of course. I mean, everyone judges everybody. You can't help but form impressions. But you can be—well, tactful. I don't think he's very tactful."

"He seems tactful enough to me."

"It's not tact, then. I don't know what it is. I just sense it."

"Well, it's nice to see Lyle with someone again."

"He's all wrong for Lyle. It won't last."

"Of course it won't last. That's why you should be nice to him. It's just something Lyle's going through."

"It makes me miss Tony so much."

"We all miss Tony. Do you mean for this to boil?"

"Is it boiling? No. Turn it down."

Robert closed the door. He looked at the framed prints

of ornamental fowl hanging on the wall. He read their names to himself: White-faced Black Spanish, Brown-breasted Red Game, Black Frizzled Fowl. After a while Lyle came up and embraced him from behind. When Robert did not respond, Lyle asked, "What's the matter?"

Robert turned around and looked at Lyle. His hair was wet and slicked to his head. His shaved face was smooth and colored from the sun. "What's the matter?" Lyle repeated.

"Do you like me?" Robert asked.

"I adore you," said Lyle. "I thought I'd just illustrated that fact most convincingly." He nodded toward the yellow room, and then leaned forward and kissed Robert. "Of course I like you," he said. "What kind of question is that? I far more than like you." He opened the door, and they went downstairs, together, to dinner.

18

The master bedroom suite in Laura's house was quite luxurious. The bathroom was large and had its own balcony. Laura lay in the aquamarine-colored tub, smoking a cigarette, looking out the open glass doors at trees and sky. She could hear the murmuring voices of Nina and

Anders from below. After a while she opened the drain and felt the water fall around her body, the last of it sucking itself into a whirlpool beneath her toes. She got out of the tub and patted herself with a towel, combed her damp hair back from her face, anointed herself with perfume and powder, put on her robe, and walked into the bedroom. She looked out the window. Anders and Nina were in the pool. Anders had his back up against the coping and Nina was straddling him, with one hand on the flagstones at either side of his head.

The sun had sunk behind the trees but there seemed to be a lot of light left outside, although everything that had been vividly colored at noon was now slurred toward gray or brown. Some birds Laura couldn't identify were noisily flying from the top of the house to the trees and back again, as if unsure of where they wanted to spend the night. She thought of the fields below her villa, and the ravens that rose up from them at this time of day, cawing off into the woods. Wherever you went in the world, there were some things that remained constant: the way the sun sank, and evening bloomed; the way birds flirted with dusk.

Below her, Nina and Anders were kissing. Long kisses. No: one kiss that went on and on, reinventing itself.

She turned away from the window. Her clothes were laid out on the bed: a black skirt, a white silk blouse. She dressed and then stood in front of the mirror, brushed her hair again, put on her jewelry. She stood for another moment, assembled, observing herself in the mirror, the dim room fading around her, her reflection fading a little more quickly. She felt hollow, and stunned. She had hoped the bath would consolidate, or reinvigorate, her spirit, but it had not. She would have to fake it.

She went down to the kitchen and put a candle, a bottle of wine, and three glasses on a tray, and carried them out to the pool. Anders was swimming laps, thrashing through the water; Nina was pouring charcoal into the hibachi.

"I thought it was time for an aperitif," said Laura. She put the tray down on the table, lit the candle, and began to uncork the wine.

"Don't you have to leave?" asked Nina.

"Not for a few minutes," said Laura. "I'm Italian. I'm supposed to be late." She waited for Nina to contradict her, but she did not. Laura poured wine into one glass and then lifted another, held it out toward Nina. "Yes?" she said.

"Please," said Nina.

Laura filled the second glass. She handed it to Nina. "I hope that little thing works," she said, nodding toward the hibachi.

"It should," said Nina.

Anders was swimming more and more slowly. The two women sipped their wine and watched him. "He seems very nice," Laura said. "Anders." She nodded at his submerged form, as if there were many Anders lurking about.

"Yes," said Nina. "He is." After a moment she added, "He's married." She said this without expression, and Laura was unsure if it was meant to corroborate or contradict his niceness.

"It's been my experience that the nicest men are always married," said Laura.

"Yes," said Nina, "but you never let that stop you."

"No," said Laura. "Not if it didn't stop them. Is his wife in the Netherlands?"

"No," said Nina. "Santa Monica."

"Well, that's just as far away."

"It's not really a matter of distance," said Nina.

"No," said Laura. "I suppose not." She was determined to ignore Nina's grudge, but she wondered how long Nina would hold it. Holding grudges makes you ugly, she almost said, but then thought better, for in Nina's case it certainly wasn't true.

Nina lit a match and held it to the newspaper she had bedded beneath the charcoal. She stepped back and watched it burn. Anders pulled himself out of the pool. He stood panting and dripping on the flagstones. His bathing suit was slicked tight to his skin, articulating his penis. He noticed them both looking at it and tugged at the material.

Laura put her empty glass of wine down on the table. "Well, I'd better be on my way," she said. "I hope you two have a nice dinner. I shouldn't be home so awfully late."

"Take your time," said Nina.

"Have a nice evening," said Anders.

"Damn," said Nina. The fire had gone out but the charcoal hadn't lit. "Do you have any lighter fluid?" she asked.

"No," said Laura.

"I'll do it," said Anders.

Laura stood there. She felt she shouldn't leave until the barbecue was properly functioning. "Is there anything I can do?" she asked.

Nina looked up at her from where she knelt beside the hibachi. "No," she said. "Go."

As Laura walked around the house toward the driveway, she heard Nina laugh. She's laughing at me, Laura thought. This made her feel so sad she stopped walking. She decided not to go to dinner. She'd stay with Nina and Anders. If it meant that much to Nina, which obviously it did, it was the right thing to do. In fact, it was rather sweet of Nina to be so upset. She'd call Marian Kerr and say she felt sick. Or her car wouldn't start. Something. She turned around and walked toward the pool. Anders and Nina were standing on the lawn, kissing. Anders had taken his bathing suit off. Nina had removed her shirt. Their discarded clothes lay in a little heap on the grass. They had relit the hibachi with more newspaper and Laura watched the flames attack the air. Bits of spark-embroidered newspaper flew up into the dark.

19

John was putting Roland to bed. Roland lay in his crib, looking up at the ceiling disappearing into the gloom. His eyes were wide open, focused, but his gaze did not shift. He was staring intently and passionlessly. At what? He looked as if he knew everything or nothing. "Roland," John said. Roland moved his head so that he was looking at John. "You're fine," John said out loud. "Aren't you?"

Roland did not respond. John leaned over and touched one of his fingers against Roland's clean, cool, soft cheek. Roland's eyes narrowed, almost imperceptibly, in concentration. "Are you fine?" John asked. Roland's eyes relaxed. In that way, he smiled. It was just a matter of degrees, of setting one thing against another. And this expression, compared to that other, was a smile. John continued to stroke Roland's cheek. The ceiling was gone. The walls rose up into cool, fluid darkness.

John heard a car coming up the driveway and looked out the window. It was a little red sports car. It pulled up onto the lawn in front of the house as if it were in a TV commercial. The woman Marian had invited to dinner got out. She stood on the lawn for a moment, smoothing first her skirt and then her hair. All smoothed, she looked up at the underside of the trees, and then reached inside the open car window and grabbed a pack of cigarettes from the dashboard. She pulled the wrapper off the pack and tossed it back into the car. She was trying to light a cigarette when John heard the front door open. So did the woman. She pushed the cigarettes into her pocketbook and looked up toward the house.

"Oh, good," he heard Marian call out, "you've brought a sweater. I was going to give you a call and suggest it, as we're eating outside."

"I'd hoped so," said the woman. She walked up the front steps. "I'm sorry I'm so dreadfully late. My daughter appeared today, up from New York, and that slowed things down a bit."

"Why didn't you bring her?" asked Marian.

"Oh, she's here with her fiancé," said the woman. Then the front door closed.

John didn't want to go downstairs. He wondered when—and if—he would be missed. Marian would come up after a while. But it would be a while. They would miss the fact of him before they missed him. John didn't like socializing. He knew that theoretically people were interesting, and he was sure that the woman who parked her car on his lawn was interesting. Marian was very good at finding interesting people. But John didn't really like interesting people. They made him feel even duller than he usually felt. His mother used to call him a dullard. She said it often; she liked the word. She was always urging him to cultivate what she called "high spirits." She said life was too short not to do exactly what you wanted. *Exactly*. She was incredibly selfish but somehow by embracing and celebrating her selfishness she had managed to convert it to charm. And yet his mother had not been happy. She cried all the time. John remembered her in Rome: she lay on the couch in the middle of the afternoon with the drapes drawn and sobbed.

The woman who had come to dinner reminded him of his mother. His mother would have driven her car up onto the lawn. Always doing something to say I am here, look at me. I don't park there, with everyone else. I park here. I park wherever I want.

Tony was not a dullard. Tony had high spirits—forceful and contagious. They transcended awkwardness and enlivened a party or a meal or simply a conversation. If Tony was present at a party something invariably happened: people danced or sang or skinny-dipped or put on pageants or played games. Things got thrown or broken, and in the midst of this furor John was able to relax. It was easy to disappear with Tony around. If Tony were downstairs, John would not hesitate to descend. But Tony was dead.

"John, you remember Laura Ponti, don't you?"

"Of course," said John. He walked down the back steps. They were all sitting around the table in the garden. Marian was pouring glasses of white wine. "It's nice to see you again." He shook her hand.

"I was just saying what a lovely house you have," said Laura. "And you're on a river. Can you swim in it?"

"Yes," said Marian. "You'll have to come over one afternoon."

"I'd adore a swim," said Laura. "I have a pool at my place, but there's something about a pool I find so depressing. It takes all the natural pleasure out of bathing, I think."

"Well," said Marian, lifting her glass. "To summertime?"

They all echoed her toast.

"It's so nice to meet you, Lyle," said Laura. "I read the review of your new book in the *Times* and tried to buy a copy, but the bookstores up here are hopeless. Supposedly the one in Woodstock has ordered me a copy. I do so wish I'd had it for this evening, though, so you could sign it. I have quite a collection of signed first editions."

"I've got some extra copies," said Marian. "I'll have him sign one for you before you leave."

"That would be splendid," said Laura. "How long are you up here for, Lyle?"

"Just for the weekend," said Lyle. "We go back to the city tomorrow."

"We?"

"Yes," said Lyle. "I'm up here with Robert."

"Oh!" said Laura. "Of course. I thought—well, never

mind what I thought. Although I'm sure I don't know why you aren't staying up here longer. I went down to the city last week, to see some friends for lunch. It seemed quite pointless. Everyone so hot and cross and the dirty air sticking to you. And can you still take taxis in the city? I found the experience very unpleasant. But you see, I don't think cities are meant for summer. I suppose it's elitist of me, but I really think people are supposed to go away for the summer."

"If everyone went away, then wouldn't the country be crowded?" asked Robert.

"Yes, but there's more room between people in the country. You adjust to it. It takes a while, though, don't you think? You have to get rid of that awful urban energy. It's so negative. My daughter came up today from the city and nearly drove me crazy. She was wound up tight as . . . is it drum? Tight as a drum? I don't see why. It gets so confusing to use figures of speech when you speak several languages. They get all jumbled up somehow, and make no sense."

"How long is your daughter up for?" asked Marian.

"Oh, just the weekend. She's filming a movie in the city. I had rented the house so she could come up every weekend, but you know how it is on film sets, she hasn't managed to get away until now."

"What movie is it?" asked Robert.

"I don't know what it's called. I started out seeing all her movies, but they were so awful I had to stop."

"What other movies has she been in?" asked Robert.

"I don't know. Actually I do, but I'm too embarrassed to tell you."

"Well, it's nice she finally made it up," said Marian.

"I suppose so," said Laura, "but in a way it's so disturbing. To have someone just for the weekend. They breeze in and disrupt everything, and before you can adjust they're gone."

"I hope all weekend guests aren't like that," said Lyle.

"If you mean you, of course not," said Marian. She laughed. "But you're not a guest, Lyle. You're family."

"I should think of Nina that same way, but I don't. I suppose it's my living so far away, and only seeing her occasionally."

"That's a shame," said Marian. "You must be disappointed."

Laura looked for a moment at the stain her lipstick had made on the wineglass. "No," she said. "Not at all." She realized this comment required some explanation. "I think there's a romantic notion of family intimacy that's . . . well, just that: a notion."

"What do you mean?" asked Robert.

Laura looked at him. "I mean I think children are meant to grow up and away from parents. I think this idea of maintaining a lifelong unit is unnatural and sentimental. Economics and religion have warped our perception of how families should really function."

"How do you think families should function?" asked Robert.

"Oh, I think, well obviously, if you're going to have children, you've got to raise them. That's the real curse on women. But don't think they owe you anything. If you think they do, if you think they're going to attend to you in your dotage, you're hopelessly naïve. It's not the way of the world. People should get together when they need one another. Beyond that, I don't think we're obligated."

"But needing isn't always mutual," said Marian. "And of course we aren't obligated to love one another, but we do, don't we, in families, and don't we want to be near to and attend to those we love?"

"I don't think we always love one another in families," said Robert. "That hasn't been my experience, at least."

"It's another one of those notions," said Laura. "Ideally, we do, of course. But it's been my experience that familial relationships seem to always fall short of the ideal. I've found them to be pretty similar to all other relationships. People grow up and change. And there's

nothing wrong or tragic in that. It's perfectly natural."
She took a sip of her wine and realized she had somehow
finished it all. She leaned forward and put the glass down
on the table. "I think I'll visit the ladies' room before we
eat," she said.

"It's right off the kitchen, in the hall," said Marian.

Laura stood up. It had gotten dark while they sat there.
She looked up toward the house, and the bright eyes of
its windows looked back at her.

"John, why don't you go up and put on the garden
lights," said Marian.

John got up and went into the house. Lights appeared,
one near each of the steps, and Laura climbed them.
John held the kitchen door open for her and pointed
toward the bathroom. It was one of those horrible bath-
rooms built in under the stairs, just a sink and a toilet,
no window, the ceiling sloped at an acute angle. Laura
stood for a moment looking in the small mirror. An arch
of leaves was etched in the glass above her face. She could
hear Marian and John in the kitchen talking in low, confident, hostessy tones. What was I saying? she wondered.
She knew she wasn't drunk but she felt as if she were,
as if her behavior were a step or two ahead of her consciousness. Just calm down, she told herself. Calm down.

* * *

"And what do you do, Robert?" Laura asked, when they had all returned to the table and were eating the grilled fish.

"Mainly answer questions about what I do," said Robert. "At least since I met Lyle."

"And when did you meet Lyle?"

"A few weeks ago," said Robert.

"Well, we met first at Skowhegan," said Lyle. "That was over a month ago."

"Recently, at any event," said Laura. "No wonder you seem so happy together. There is nothing more wonderful than falling in love. That is why I have done it so many times."

"How many?" asked Robert. He had the feeling this woman was trying to be scandalous, or at least entertaining, and that no one was really encouraging her.

"What a question to ask a woman! Fortunately, I have no shame. I have been in love—I have loved—eleven times. And married four times."

"Are you in love now?" asked Robert.

"Not with a man. Or a woman, for that matter. Now I am in love with my villa, and my life there. And it is the best love I have ever known. I have discovered that people should always love where they live. If they don't, they should move. The world is very big in that way. Do you agree?"

"But most people can't afford to move somewhere just because they want to," said Robert.

"Of course not," said Laura. "I do not allow economic reality to affect much of what I say. I find it boring. But you agree with me, theoretically, at least?"

"I don't know," said Robert. "I think people are more important than places. I would rather love people."

"By all means, do. I'm not discouraging that. But a good house somewhere, like this one"—and she motioned behind her—"that is the thing to love most: real estate. Because it won't leave you, or change. You can leave, or change it, but it won't leave you. It's truly yours."

"It can't hold you," said Robert. "Or talk to you, or understand you."

"If you think that, you haven't spent time in the right house," said Laura. "At night, when I am alone in my house, I feel held by it, and talked to, and understood. In fact, far better than by some men. Most men."

"I think the thing is to have the house full of people you love," said Marian. "That, to me, is ideal."

"But then the house isn't really yours," said Laura.

"Yes it is," said Marian, "but sharing it makes it better."

"But you can share things and still possess them," said Laura. "That is the best. To share them, not give them away. People give away too much, and then regret it."

"I don't think you can ever give too much away to those you love," said Marian.

"That is because you're basically a kind and lovely person. I am not. I was once. But it is very hard to retain that. At least it was for me. I always try to be kind, but my personality interferes. Kindness is a quality that gets worn down by the years, I think. You end up with a little patina of kindness, an aura of goodness, but not the thing itself. That's why I'm always fascinated when I meet an older person who is truly kind. They're angels, I think. Saints. But so few. That's one reason why I like young people so much. You, for instance"—she nodded at Robert—"you who want to love people and not buildings, it does my heart good to hear you say that, to know those feelings still exist in the world."

"People usually think I'm very cynical," said Robert.

"Well, I don't think you can be alive today without being cynical. Unless you're an idiot. Cynicism is our second nature. But it's just an armor; it only covers our true nature. And it is not, I think, very thick on you. What *do* you do? You may be tired of the question, but I'm curious. Now that I've taken an interest in you."

"I'm working in a restaurant," said Robert. "And trying to be a painter."

"Do you know how to restore paintings?"

"No," said Robert.

"I do," said Marian. "Why?"

"Do you?" asked Laura. "I didn't know that. How interesting."

"I used to work for the Met," said Marian.

"Have you ever restored frescoes?"

"No," said Marian. "Just canvases."

John stood up. "Excuse me," he said, "but I just remembered I left the sprinkler on in the garden. I'll be right back."

"I don't hear it," said Marian.

They were all quiet for a second, listening for the sprinkler.

"It's on very softly," said John. He walked down the lawn, into the darkness.

"Pretty soon he's going to start sleeping in the garden," said Marian.

"Then let him," said Laura. "One thing I've learned is that you've got to let men sleep wherever they want."

No one—not even Robert—seemed prepared to respond to this comment. "What were you saying before, about frescoes?" asked Lyle.

"Oh," said Laura. "Well, I'm having a lot of restoration done in my villa, and I was having some walls replastered. These awful Brits owned the house before me and did it all up with Laura Ashley. Can you imagine: Laura Ashley in a villa?"

"No," said Lyle, who thought even rhetorical questions about aesthetics should be answered.

"Of course not," continued Laura. "Anyway, underneath the wallpaper in the music room we discovered frescoes. Of course they're badly damaged, but I'd like to have them restored."

"I could get some names for you, I'm sure," said Marian.

"Could you? They're probably second-rate and not worth the effort—or expense—but I'd feel awful if I didn't at least have someone look at them. Plus the government, these days, is impossible. You can hardly clean out a closet without their permission."

John heard the rasp of the pine trees and footsteps. Lyle appeared through the hedge, looking toward the garden.

"There you are," said Lyle. "Marian sent me to retrieve you. Are you all right? Is anything wrong?"

John walked toward the garden fence, near Lyle. "No," he said.

"Good," said Lyle. "It's a lovely night. I like your guest. She's very entertaining."

"She's a little crazy, I think."

"The most entertaining people always are," said Lyle.

"She talks too much."

"And you talk too little," said Lyle. "So it all evens out. What are you doing here? Was the sprinkler on?"

"No," said John.

"We should go back," said Lyle. "I think Marian's concerned."

"About what?"

"About what Marian is always concerned with: that things go well."

"Aren't things going well?" asked John.

"As far as I'm concerned, they are," said Lyle. "I'm having a wonderful weekend. I'm happy to be here."

"Is Robert?"

"Yes," said Lyle.

"Maybe we can go swimming later, in the dark."

"I think it's too cold."

"Perhaps Robert will. He likes to swim."

"Ask him. Let's go back." Lyle wanted to get back. It made him nervous to stand alone with John in the dark. They had never really talked about—or acknowledged—

Tony's death, and Lyle had the feeling that John, at any moment, might. It took such a long time for things to bubble up through John; one never knew when—if—they might surface. "Let's go back," Lyle repeated. He pushed himself through the hedge. He stood on the other side and looked up the lawn. He could see the candles, and the faces around them. "Are you coming?" he called back to John.

"Yes," said John.

When the meal was finished, Marian stood up and began stacking plates.

"Let me help you," said Robert, standing up as well.

"No, no," said Marian. "Sit down."

John and Lyle and Laura were seated. Laura was smoking a thin brown cigarette, exhaling drifts of smoke over her shoulder into the darkness. "No," said Robert. "I'll help." He wanted to hurt Marian in some way, and helping her when she did not want help was the best way he knew. They carried the dishes up the terraced steps to the house. They paused at the kitchen door, both of their hands full. "Here," said Robert, shifting his load, reaching out for the door. He dropped a plate on the bricks. The sound of it smashing seemed very loud.

"Oh no," he said. "I'm sorry."

"Just get the door," said Marian. "It's nothing. No—don't try to pick it up. I'll get the broom."

John appeared behind them. He opened the door and took some dishes from them both.

They piled the dishes in the sink. The light in the kitchen seemed unusually bright and artificial after the candlelit gloom of the back yard. Robert began to rinse the plates under the tap, but Marian said, "Leave them, please. Join the others."

"Are you sure I can't help?"

"I'll give you a shout when I'm ready with the dessert," said Marian. She actually pushed him a little.

Back at the table, Laura was drawing the floor plan of her villa on a blank page of her Filofax. Then she drew another of how it would be when the renovation was complete. The bathroom floors, she announced, were to be sheathed in anodized aluminum.

Marian came down the steps sideways, balancing a large platter to one side of her. Everyone stopped talking and watched her descend, as if she were a Ziegfeld girl. She waited for Laura to remove her sketch, and then laid the platter in the middle of the table. A pyramid of lacy, nearly transparent cookies was surrounded by grapes.

The grapes were red, their underbellies flushed lime green.

Robert could feel Lyle's bare foot caressing the muscle of his calf beneath the table, but Lyle was not looking at him. He was smoking one of Laura's cigarettes, and in the way he held and inhaled the cigarette Robert could tell he had once been a smoker. Lyle's arm was extended along the back of Laura's chair, inches from her bare neck. He was not flirting, Robert knew, but simply being charming.

Robert reached out and tugged at a bunch of grapes, plucking one from its thin stem, so that just a touch of its moist insides remained behind on the stalk.

"Oh, Robert, here," said Marian. She picked up a pair of heavy, ornate scissors and held them toward Robert. They glowed in the candlelight.

Robert put the grape into his mouth, and held it there, intact. He was confused.

"They're grape scissors," Marian said. "You use these to cut a small bunch of grapes, instead of pulling them off one by one." She demonstrated this phenomenon, and then held the scissors toward Robert.

Robert did not take the scissors.

The moment seemed very long: Marian's extended

hand, offering the scissors; the grape, round and cool in Robert's mouth; all of their dumb faces touched with candlelight.

"Oh, don't tame him!" Laura suddenly cried. "Let him eat grapes with his fingers if he wants! Let us all be free of these stupid affectations!" She grabbed the scissors from Marian and flung them over her shoulder.

No one moved. It was quiet except for the drone of the insects and the chafe of the leaves in the trees, which hovered above them in great dark clouds. Finally Laura laughed a little, but to herself. She pushed back her chair, got up, and retrieved the scissors from where they lay on the lawn. She placed them on the table. Everyone looked at them. They were lovely: chased silver, each loop a trellis of engraved vines.

Marian touched them. "They were my grandmother's," she said.

20

After dinner, Lyle and Robert went for a walk along the river. Once the lights from the house had faded behind them, it was quite dark. "What river is this?" asked Robert.

"I don't know," said Lyle. "I don't think I've heard it referred to by name."

"Where does it flow?"

"It flows—well, I assume into the Hudson. Let's see." Lyle paused to consider directions, but had trouble orienting himself in the darkness. And the river twisted so. "I'm sure it flows into the Hudson. All rivers around here must. It's a tributary."

"Which do you like better," asked Robert, "rivers or lakes? Or ponds?"

"Rivers, I think. I like the idea of the water constantly moving. There's something stagnant—in comparison—about lakes and ponds."

The path narrowed and they had to continue in single file. Robert went ahead. They walked for a moment without talking, and then Lyle asked, "What did you think of our dinner guest? Signora Ponti?"

"I liked her," said Robert. "I thought she was funny."

"Yes," said Lyle, "she was. In a self-dramatizing fashion."

"Didn't you like her?"

"Oh, yes, she was good company for a dinner. I just think she was trying a bit too hard. It's a little tragic: glamorous women at that age. They get desperate. Flinging the grape scissors. That kind of thing."

"I liked her," said Robert.

"That's because she came to your defense," said Lyle. Robert didn't respond.

"Are you upset about the scissors?" asked Lyle.

"No," said Robert.

"Oh. I thought perhaps you were."

"No," said Robert. "I'm upset, but that's not it."

"Then what is it?"

"Do you really want to know?"

"Of course I do. Tell me."

"They think I'm all wrong for you," Robert said.

"What?" asked Lyle. "Who?"

"John and Marian. They think I'm wrong for you."

"No they don't," said Lyle. He held his hand out a ways in front of him, for he was having trouble seeing in the darkness. Robert, judging by how quickly he was walking, was not.

"Yes they do," said Robert.

"Do you mean about the scissors? That was just Marian being Marian. You'll get used to it. Slow down a little. This isn't a race."

"I don't mean about the scissors. The scissors were stupid."

"Then what do you mean?"

"I heard them talking and saying they didn't like me and they don't think I'm right for you and that we won't last."

Lyle took this opportunity to stop walking and said, rather stupidly, "What? Were you eavesdropping?"

"Yes," said Robert.

"Where? When?"

"At the top of the stairs. Before dinner."

"You shouldn't have been."

"Why?"

"Because it's wrong. It's impolite."

"Like eating grapes without scissors?"

"No," said Lyle. "That's different."

"How's it different?"

"That's culturally impolite, it's simply a question of manners, while eavesdropping is—well, it's intrinsically impolite."

"How can something be intrinsically impolite?"

"Some things can," said Lyle. He paused. "Murder, for instance."

"I didn't murder anyone," said Robert. "I just opened a door and overheard a conversation."

"I know," said Lyle. "I just wish you hadn't listened."

Robert shrugged. "I did."

"Well, you shouldn't take to heart what you weren't meant to hear. That's a good rule."

"I think just the opposite," said Robert. "I think things you weren't meant to hear are often the most important. Nobody tells you things directly."

"That's not true," said Lyle.

"I'm beginning to think it is," said Robert.

"Well, you're wrong. You shouldn't make such a big deal out of this."

"I didn't think mentioning it to you was making a big deal."

Lyle considered this for a moment. "You're right," he said. "It's not. So can't we just forget it?"

"You can forget it, if you want." Robert turned and began to walk along the path.

"Wait," said Lyle. "And what about you?"

Robert stopped, but remained facing away. "What about me?" he asked.

"Can you forget it?" asked Lyle. "At least until we leave?"

Robert turned around. "No," he said. "I can't. It makes me feel very awkward. In fact, I don't think I really want to stay here."

"Well, it's the middle of the night. Where are you going to go?"

"I don't know," said Robert. "Nowhere. I just want you to know how I felt. How I feel."

"Well, I'm glad you told me. I'm sorry, but I'm sure you misheard them. I know John and Marian. They wouldn't say something like that about you. In fact, I happen to know that they both like you. They told me so themselves, this afternoon."

"Well, I know what I heard," said Robert.

"What did you hear? What did they say?"

"What I told you. They said—Marian said she didn't like me. And then they agreed I was all wrong for you and that we wouldn't last very long because your seeing me was just a phase you were going through. Part of your. . . ."

"Part of my what?"

"Your mourning, I think. Your healing."

Lyle was finding it difficult to concentrate. He irrationally wished it was less dark; he felt he could think more clearly if he could just see more of what surrounded them. He also wished he had not drunk as much wine as he had with dinner. "That's nonsense," he managed to say. "People often conjecture about other people's relationships, privately, but that doesn't mean that they're right."

"So you think they're wrong?"

"About what?"

"About what Marian said." Robert sounded exasperated. "Do you think I'm right for you?"

"Right and wrong—I think it's premature to think in those terms. I think it's immature. I think," Lyle said, "that at this point in my life no one is right for me."

"Was Tony right for you?"

Lyle looked out at the river.

"Was he?" Robert insisted.

Right? thought Lyle. What a stupid, romantic notion. Yet at moments Tony had been right. At moments it had hurt, and it hurt more now, when Tony was dead, for it had been an odd, unnoticeable rightness that had quietly staked its territories in Lyle's heart, had followed his rivers to their sources, and left flags there, high in the uncharted parts of him. "Yes," he said. "In some ways— many ways—Tony was right."

"And I'm not."

"I didn't say that, Robert. I don't really know you yet. What I know of you I like very much, but I know so little. I think this whole conversation is foolish."

"But if you had to guess."

"I would never want to guess about something as important as that."

"But do you know what you're doing?"

"Do I what?"

"Do you know what you're doing with me? Or are you just fucking around?"

"What am I doing with you? I'm trying to have a relationship. That's what I'm *trying* to do. I'm not fucking around. But I think your forcing me to answer these stupid questions is a ridiculous thing. That's fucking around with me."

"No," said Robert. "You don't understand. Maybe I'm not saying it right. All I'm asking is if you can imagine our relationship developing. Can you imagine our loving one another? Because I can imagine that. Can you?"

"As you know, I have trouble imagining anything about my future," said Lyle. "Besides, why is that so important: if I can imagine something or not? Just because I can imagine something doesn't mean it's going to happen."

"No," said Robert. "But it helps. It's encouraging."

"Well, I don't want to encourage you unreasonably."

"Oh," said Robert.

"Is that what you want? Do you want me to lie to you, and tell you things that aren't true?"

"No," said Robert. "I want you to tell me the truth. Am I just a part of your healing? What are we doing here? What am I doing here?"

Lyle looked around them, as if Robert meant this specific place. There was very little he could see except for Robert, whose white shirt—it was one of his waiter's shirts, Lyle supposed—and eyes stood apart from the general darkness of trees and river and sky. Lyle stared at him for a moment, long enough so that the parts of Robert obscured by darkness became visible. "What are we doing here?" he said. "I'll tell you what I think we're doing here. We're two people who met one another. Who, I thought, found one another attractive. Who like one another's company. And so we came away together for a weekend, to spend some time together. That is what I thought we were doing here. I didn't think it was so very complicated."

"Maybe not for you," said Robert.

"Well, of course it's complicated," said Lyle. "I told you it would be, I told you what the situation is."

"On the train," said Robert.

"Yes," said Lyle, "on the train. I'm sorry about that. I should have told you sooner. I thought about it, I tried to, but I couldn't. I'm sorry."

He paused. Robert was looking down at the ground. "Let's go back now, and go to bed and forget about this for a while. Today was a difficult day, for everybody. Tomorrow will be different."

"You sound like what's her name," said Robert. "Scarlett O'Hara."

"It pains me to speak in clichés, but this conversation forces me to. There's no way to discuss something as inane as this rationally."

"Inane? Whether we love one other or not is inane?"

"Oh, please," said Lyle. "Love is something that—this is not about love. I'm very fond of you, Robert, you know that. I like you very much. But this is not about love."

"It is for me," said Robert.

"You don't love me," said Lyle. "I know you may think you do, but you don't."

"How do you know what I feel?" asked Robert.

"I know it sounds presumptuous, but I know you don't love me. If you loved me—if what you feel is love—love would be a very cheap and common thing."

"What I feel for you isn't cheap or common."

"I know that," said Lyle. "That's not what I meant. I meant love doesn't happen like this, real love, it doesn't occur in a few days, or weeks, or months, even. Real love is something that evolves very slowly over time."

Robert looked down at the ground for a moment, and then looked up. "I think you're just scared," he said.

"Scared?" asked Lyle. "Scared of what?"

"Scared of—if you don't love me, then why, when we made love before, did you say that you did?"

"I didn't say that," said Lyle.

"Yes," said Robert, "you did. Don't lie."

Lyle remembered: their lying together on the bed in the yellow room, their bodies merged in the golden light, how it had escaped from him, an exhalation. "Well," he said, "I believe there are some instances when one is usually forgiven for not speaking the literal truth. When one is—"

"Forget this 'one' business."

"I'm sorry," said Lyle. "When I—when we made love, I may have said I loved you—"

"You did," said Robert.

"All right, I did. But, Robert, this isn't a question of semantics. I could have said anything then."

"And you could say anything now."

"I could. Of course I could. But I'm not. Now I'm telling you the truth. Now we are standing here, we aren't making love, and I can speak more truthfully."

"What? You can't make love and speak truthfully at the same time?"

"I don't know," said Lyle. "Apparently not. But I'm speaking the truth now."

"How do I know that?"

"Because I'm telling you I am."

They stood there for a moment.

"And what are you telling me? What is the truth?"

"I'm telling you that I don't love you. Now. And, Robert, darling, that's not a terrible thing. I feel, and will come to feel, other things, other very worthwhile and wonderful things, about you. Maybe even love. I hope love. But love is—" Lyle shook his head. "You can't be so obsessed with love, Robert. It will just make you miserable."

"I am miserable," said Robert. "I feel like I'm bleeding. Like I'm losing myself."

"You're just being melodramatic," said Lyle. "You're not losing yourself. In fact, I doubt very much that you've even found yourself."

"I hate that worst of all," said Robert. "I hate when someone else tells you what's happening inside yourself."

"I'm sorry," said Lyle. "You're right. If you say you're miserable, then you are. And I am miserable you are miserable, because I have made you miserable, and that was never my intention. Do you believe that?"

"Yes," said Robert.

"Then can't we go back? And go to bed?" Lyle reached out and touched Robert's white shoulder.

"I'm not going back there," said Robert. He raised his

shoulder, slightly, so that Lyle's hand had to either grip it or fall off. It fell off.

"What do you mean?" Lyle asked.

"I mean I'm not going back to their house. I think they're awful people—Marian especially. If you think I'm going back there, you're crazy."

"Then where are you going?"

"I'm going home," said Robert.

"And how are you getting there?"

"I'll walk to the train station."

"The train station is miles from here. And I doubt very much the trains run this late."

"I have no problem walking ten miles. And I have no problem waiting for a train. I'd much rather do that than go back to the house."

"Robert," said Lyle, "don't be silly. I'm sorry if they —or I—upset you. But you can't just leave in the middle of the night. It isn't done. Come back to the house, and if you still want to leave in the morning we'll make some excuse and leave together. I promise."

"No," said Robert. "I'm leaving now. Thank you for being honest with me." He turned and walked into the dark woods purposefully, as if a trail were clearly marked to the railroad station.

Lyle tried to make himself call out, or follow, but did

neither. He felt drunk and exhausted. After a moment
he did call Robert's name, but there was no answer. He
walked a ways into the woods, trying to listen for Robert's
footsteps. He thought he could hear them, but they
sounded far away, and when he began to walk toward
them they were obscured by his own commotion. He tried
to walk more quickly. Suddenly someone swung a bat
into his face. He thought he heard himself cry out before
he felt the blow. He stood in the dark for a moment,
stunned. Then he realized he had walked into a tree. He
reached up to find his glasses were broken and what felt
like blood on his nose and lips. Stop, he thought. He
stood with one hand on his face and one hand touching
the tree. He was panting, he realized, and sobbing, his
breath coming in strange shaking gasps. He kept thinking: Stop, just stop. It was all he could think.

21

Laura Ponti had driven quite a ways before she realized
she had no idea where she was going. She was driving
without direction, just driving, concentrating on keeping
the car on the road, following the bright tunnel of her
headlights. It was partly because she was drunk, and

partly because she didn't know the roads at all well, but nevertheless, she was lost.

The road was deserted of both houses and traffic; trees crowded up along either side and touched branches overhead. There are roads that go toward, and roads that go away from, and Laura had the feeling this road was the latter. So she pulled over, and as soon as she had stopped the car, she felt much less panicked: at least she was not getting more lost. I'll just sit here awhile, she thought, and then I'll try to retrace my route. If I can find my way back to the Kerrs' I can find my way home. She tried to recollect how she had driven from her house to the Kerrs', but that trip seemed ages ago, and thinking of her house made her think of Nina, a thought she had kept successfully submerged all evening—parties were good for that kind of thing—but now that she was alone in the dark, the thought of Nina resurfaced like some buoyant, ugly fish, and she felt an awful weariness that, combined with her drunkenness, made her want to close her eyes and sleep. She turned off the engine and the lights, and watched their illumination wither. She closed her eyes.

Of course Nina was right: she was a pathetic and foolish woman. That was one of the hardest things about having a daughter, even an absent, distant daughter, like Nina:

they saw through you. Of course she saw through Nina, too. But somehow all that insight didn't add up to anything. It only served to alienate them.

She opened her eyes. She was about to start the car and turn around when she saw a figure walking down the road along the white stripe. She turned the headlights on and doused it with light. It was the boy from the dinner party: Robert. He stopped walking and covered his eyes with his hands. He looked like a child, standing in the middle of the road like that, shielding his eyes. Laura turned off her lights and opened the car door. "Robert?" she called.

"Yes," he said.

"It's me," she said. "Laura Ponti. What are you doing?"

"Walking," he said.

"Well, apparently. Where to? Could I offer you a ride?"

He approached the car and knelt down beside it. "I was going to the train station," he said. "I need to go back to the city."

"Now? Whatever for? What's happened?"

"I just decided to go back. I didn't want to stay there anymore."

"I can't say I blame you," said Laura. "Well, why don't

you get in, and I'll see if I can find the train station. I doubt I can get any more lost. How long have you been walking?''

"About fifteen minutes," said Robert. "Mostly in the woods, though. I just came out on the road up there." He crossed in front of the car and stood beside the passenger door.

"Well, get in. You've got to reach inside to open the door. That's it. I was planning to turn around, but what do you think?''

"Yes," said Robert. "I'd turn around."

Laura started the car and made a U-turn. When they had driven a little ways she said, "So you had a lovers' quarrel?''

"Yes," said Robert. "I suppose you could call it that."

"And you stormed off into the woods. Good for you! I had trouble understanding what you were doing with Lyle Wyatt.''

"I like Lyle," said Robert. "I just don't think he's ready to get involved with anyone at the moment."

"That's nonsense," said Laura. "One is always ready to fall in love. It isn't something you have to train for."

"His lover died a year ago."

"If love is meant to happen, it happens. Not even

196

mourning interferes. Personally, I've always found mourning a bit of an aphrodisiac."

Robert did not respond to this comment.

"I'm sorry. That was in poor taste," said Laura. "I only meant to say that, well, there is no excuse for not falling in love. But, nevertheless, it is disappointing when it fizzles."

"Yes," said Robert. "It is."

"And it's worst when you're young. You have no perspective."

"I have my own perspective," said Robert.

"Of course you do. How smug of me."

They drove for a while, passing nothing but trees. Laura slowed as they approached a crossroads. An amber blinking light was suspended on a sloping wire above the intersection. "Well," she said. "What do you think? Does any of this look familiar?"

"No," said Robert.

"Let's turn, then," said Laura. "When in doubt, turn."

Lyle stood for a while, trying to orient himself. He listened for the river, but heard only the rustling, slightly ornery sounds of the forest. He put his arms out in front of him, and began walking in the direction that seemed the least dark. He walked tentatively, anticipating with his fingertips the awful things in front of him.

Eventually the darkness ahead began to appear less dense, and he was able to discern the tree trunks before he touched them. And then the trees were gone and he was standing in a clearing, and there was John's wall, curved across the ground in front of him, and the river, a sort of agitated darkness, to one side.

His relief at no longer being lost was almost debilitating. He walked over to the wall and sat down on the matted grass inside one of its curves. He felt a little as if he had fainted, as if in the moments he had been absent the world had changed and left him behind. He knew that the house was on the other side of the fir trees, at the top of the lawn, but he did not want to return to it. How could he explain what had happened? What *had* happened? Robert had run away. Lyle felt sure that Robert could take care of himself. He wouldn't walk into trees. He would sidle between them. Lyle touched his face again and studied the blood on his fingers. He hadn't taken care of Robert. He could not take care of himself. Ever since Tony died. Tony had not taken care of him, but Tony's life set next to his had contained him somehow, had given his life form and function. But now his life spilled messily around him into the world. He was out of control without Tony. And Tony was dead.

A scarlet fluorescent glow materialized into the letters DINER.

"Why don't we stop here and ask directions? And get a cup of coffee, too," suggested Laura. "Real coffee."

"That sounds good," said Robert.

She pulled into the gravelly lot and parked beside several other cars. The diner was long and cylindrical, pushed up against a flight of concrete steps. They climbed these and entered. A row of booths on either side of the door was separated by a narrow aisle from the counter. They sat in a booth farthest from the door. A waitress approached with a pot of coffee and two mugs.

"Coffee?" she asked, holding the pot aloft.

"Please," said Laura.

The waitress placed the mugs on the table in front them and filled them. "Would you like to see menus?" she asked.

"I think not," said Laura.

"Pie?"

"Would you like some pie?" Laura asked Robert. "What kind do you have?"

"Peach, blueberry, and strawberry-rhubarb."

"I'll have blueberry," said Robert.

"And I'll try the strawberry-rhubarb," said Laura.

The waitress went in search of pie.

Laura sipped her coffee and made a face.

"We forgot to ask directions," said Robert.

"Yes," said Laura. "I was distracted by the pie. How nice to eat pie in the middle of the night. I adore pie," she added, as if her enthusiasm needed explanation.

"So do I," said Robert. "I hope it's good."

"I have a feeling it will be," said Laura. "Bad coffee and good pie. So what did you and Lyle argue about?"

"Oh," said Robert, "it was stupid."

"No doubt," said Laura. "But what?"

"I had heard—overheard—Marian saying that I was wrong for Lyle. That we wouldn't last. So I asked Lyle what he thought."

"And what did he say?"

"At first he wouldn't answer, but then, when I pressed him, he agreed with her."

"You shouldn't have pressed him."

"Why not? I wanted to know."

"Yes, but you see, if you hadn't pressed him, you wouldn't have had that conversation, and you'd still be together, and by the time you did have that conversation—if you were foolish enough to broach it again—his answer might have been very different. Never press someone for an answer you may not want to hear."

"I thought he would answer differently. At least I hoped he might."

"Keep your hope to yourself. People feel very intimidated by hope. Especially old people like Lyle and me. Besides, hope can be awfully boring."

"So you think I was wrong?"

"Wrong? I don't think it's a question of right and wrong, really. You obviously did what you had to do. So it was the right thing, I suppose. But don't blame Lyle. You've no one to blame but yourself."

The waitress appeared with their pie. She had also brought the pot of coffee with her.

"I shall never get to sleep now," said Laura, as she accepted a refill. "We need directions to the train station," she said to the waitress.

"What train station?" asked the waitress.

"The nearest train station. To take a train to New York," said Robert.

"It's across the river," said the waitress. "In Hudson. Turn right and take this road all the way down to the river. Turn left and go about ten miles, till you come to the bridge. Across the bridge is Hudson."

"Ten miles! Are you sure there isn't a train station closer?" asked Laura.

"Yes," said the waitress. She withdrew.

"Is that where you got off the train?" asked Laura.

"No," said Robert.

"We must be more lost than we imagined."

As Lyle walked up the lawn the back door opened and John appeared, bouncing a pool of flashlight around his feet. "Lyle?" he said.

"Yes," said Lyle. "Where are you going?"

"I thought I heard some deer. I wanted to make sure they weren't in the garden. Where's Robert?"

"He's—he's gone back to the house."

"Oh," said John. "I didn't see him."

"He probably snuck in. I told him to be quiet. I thought you'd be asleep."

"Marian is," said John. "She has a headache. I'm sorry about the thing with the grape scissors."

"It wasn't your fault," said Lyle. "It was nobody's fault."

"It was rude of Marian, I thought," said John.

"No," said Lyle. "I don't think she meant to be rude. She meant to be polite. I was just looking at your wall. It looks even better at night."

"I was thinking to build something else," said John.
"What?"

"I don't know." He pointed the flashlight up into the sky, casting a pale circle of light against the stars. "Maybe something with wood that's tall. A sort of tower of sticks."

"That sounds interesting," said Lyle.

"Hey," said John, pointing the flashlight at Lyle's face. "What's happened to you?"

Lyle put his hand up to his face. The blood felt crusty across his cheeks and chin. "I walked into a tree. It was so dark."

"You should have taken a flashlight," said John. "Are you all right?"

Lyle paused for a moment, and then said, "No. I don't think so."

John came closer and touched Lyle's face, held the flashlight closer. "It's still bleeding a little," he said. "Let's go up to the house so we can clean it."

Something about John's fingers touching his face made Lyle cry.

"What's wrong?" asked John.

Lyle wanted John to hold him but he didn't know how to make this happen. He moved toward him a little, and then said, "Hold me."

John reached out, quickly, and put his arms around

Lyle. He held him firmly, as if he were shielding him from something. He said nothing. After a moment he broke away, and keeping his arm around Lyle, he began to lead him toward the house.

"Wait," Lyle said.

John paused.

"Robert isn't up at the house," said Lyle.

"Where is he? What happened?"

"He's—we had a fight. He's gone to the train station."

"How?"

"Walking. He disappeared into the woods."

"He'll never find his way to the train station. It's miles from here. We'd better take the car and look for him. He can't have got far."

"No," said Lyle.

"What were you—how did—did you really walk into a tree? Or did Robert do that to you?"

Lyle touched his face. "No It was a tree. I was trying to follow him and walked right into it. I've lost my glasses," he said. "They must have fallen off."

"We'll find them tomorrow," said John. "Let's go get you cleaned up and then look for Robert."

"I think maybe—I mean, if I go with you, and we find him, he might not—would you mind going by yourself?

I don't think he wants to see me again. And if you find him, you could drive him to the train station."

"But the trains don't run this late. And tomorrow's Sunday. The first one's not till 8:00."

"Oh," said Lyle. "Of course."

"But I'll go," said John. "And if I find him I'll bring him back here. And then I'll get up early and drive him to the station."

"This is all so stupid," said Lyle. "I've made such a mess. I'm sorry."

"Don't worry about it," said John. "Let's just get your face cleaned up."

They began to walk toward the house. "Would you do me one more favor?" Lyle asked.

"Of course," said John. "What?"

"Don't tell Marian about this," said Lyle.

"What do you mean? She'll think it's strange that Robert's just disappeared."

"I'll tell her something," said Lyle. "Tomorrow."

Marian was not asleep. She was sitting up in bed, waiting. John had gone out with the flashlight to check his garden half an hour ago and had not yet returned. Neither had Lyle or Robert. There was something unsettling about their collective absence. What was happening out there? Finally Marian heard what she assumed to be Lyle and Robert return. But then she heard the strangest thing: the car. Someone started the car and drove away. She got out of bed and walked down the long hall, around the corner, and toward the yellow room. A stripe of light lay on the floor beneath the door. She stood for a moment, but heard nothing. She knocked.

"Yes?" Lyle said.

"Lyle? It's Marian. Is everything all right?"

"Yes," said Lyle.

"Was that John who drove away?"

"Yes," said Lyle.

"Do you know where he went?"

There was a pause. "Laura Ponti left her house keys here. He went to return them."

"Oh," said Marian. "How did he know?"

"How did he know what?"

"That she left her keys here."

"I don't know. I suppose she called."

"I didn't hear the phone," said Marian.

"Perhaps you were asleep. Or maybe she didn't call. Maybe John just found them. He said he'd be right back."

"All right, then. I'm sorry to have bothered you. I was just curious. Did you have a nice walk?"

"Yes," said Lyle. "Good night."

"Good night. Good night, Robert."

Robert did not answer. Marian stood for a moment outside the door. She put her hand up against it, as if she could intuit through her touch what was happening inside. After a moment the light went out. There was silence. She had the feeling that someone—Lyle—was standing on just the other side of the door, as still and quiet as she.

The farm stand was closed, the bins outside emptied but full of moonlight. Laura gave a little shriek as they drove past it, and stopped the car.

"What?" asked Robert.

"I know where I am!" she exclaimed. "That's my farm stand. I live near here. Listen: why don't you come spend the night at my place? There isn't going to be a train for ages, and that's assuming we find the damned station. I've got a spare room and you can spend the night and meet my daughter the movie star. Actually, you can get a ride back to the city with her. I assume she'll go back the way she came. How does that sound?"

"It's very nice of you," said Robert. "But—"

"But what?"

"But. Well, I think I'd like to just get back to the city

as quickly as possible. I don't mind waiting at the station."

"But it may be hours!"

"I don't mind. Really, I don't. In fact, I'd like to. I'd like to be alone for a while."

"I think you're crazy," said Laura.

"I know," said Robert. "Listen, I don't want to take you any farther out of your way. I can walk to the station from here."

"Nonsense," said Laura. "Although I hate to abet you in this foolishness, I won't allow you to walk. We've no idea how far it really is." She started the car. "Now, you're sure about this?"

Robert nodded.

They drove away from the farm stand. After a moment Laura said, "Since I'm being nice enough to drive you to the train station, I hope you'll allow me to offer you some advice."

"What?" asked Robert.

Laura looked over at him, and then looked back at the road. "Don't feel so sorry for yourself," she said. "Feeling sorry for yourself is unavoidable, but it's the biggest waste of time. It gets you nowhere. I speak from experience in this matter."

"I don't feel sorry for myself," said Robert.

"Yes, you do," said Laura. She said it as if she were

offering a fact rather than a judgment. "You're planning to spend a mournful mopey night at the train station. Just don't mope for too long."

Robert said nothing. He looked down at his hands.

"I say these things to you because I like you," said Laura. "I like you. I'm not afraid to tell you that. People waste time in this regard, too. You are by far one of the more interesting people I've met this whole godforsaken summer."

Robert smiled a little, and shrugged.

"I can tell that there is more to you than meets the eye," Laura continued. "And I am sure that is what attracted Herr Wyatt to you. That and your good looks, of course. You are very good-looking. I am an excellent judge of these things. And Wyatt may be a fuddy-duddy but he's not stupid. Not by any means."

The bridge appeared on the right. It rose up over a river of fog. They were the only car on it. "Thank you," said Robert.

"You are welcome," said Laura.

"I like you, too," said Robert. "You're very smart and nice."

"It's funny you should say that. I'd come to a different conclusion about myself this evening."

A sign in the center of town pointed to the train station.

Laura pulled into the deserted parking lot. "It doesn't look very promising," she said.

"No," said Robert.

"You can change your mind."

"I know," said Robert. He made no move to get out of the car. "I enjoyed this very much," he said, "driving around with you. And the pie. Thanks."

"Yes," said Laura. "So did I. It was fun, in a way, wasn't it?"

"Yes," said Robert.

Laura tapped the steering wheel with her fingers for a moment. "I'm going to ask you a question," she said. "Will you answer it honestly?"

"I'll try," said Robert.

"You said you were a painter. Are you a good painter?"

"I don't know," said Robert.

"You must have some idea. Do you think you're a good painter?"

It took Robert a moment to say, "Yes. I think I am."

"Then I am going to make you an offer. Remember my frescoes that want restoring?"

"Yes," said Robert.

"Why don't you come and do it? I would very much like to have you do it."

"I don't know how to restore frescoes," said Robert.

"You could learn. I'm sure you could. They've already been ruined by Laura Ashley. You could only improve them."

"Do you mean come to Italy?"

"It would be rather difficult to do it from here," said Laura.

"I've never been to Italy," said Robert.

"It isn't a prerequisite."

"When?"

"Whenever. Think about it. Sooner than later. I'll pay you, of course. And there's a little apartment for you in the cottage. I live in the most beautiful villa in Italy. The nice thing about Italy is just about everyone can say that truthfully. Will you think about it?"

"Yes," said Robert. "Of course."

"All right, then, get out. Get out and wait for your train. I'm going home." She opened her purse and extracted a silver card case. "Here's my card," she said. "I'll be back in Italy in September. Get in touch with me. Whatever you decide, get in touch with me. Let me know the train came, if nothing else." She handed him the card.

"Thank you," said Robert. "I will." He got out of the car. "And thank you for the ride."

"It was my pleasure," said Laura. "Good night."

* * *

The house was completely dark when Laura finally returned. She drank a tall glass of water at the kitchen sink. Everything in the kitchen was clean and neat. Nina had done a very nice job of cleaning. All the surfaces were shining, everything arranged, even the fruit in the bowl neatly pyramided.

In the order, Laura intuited a truce.

She turned out the light and walked down the hall toward her bedroom. The door to Nina's room was ajar. Laura closed it, quietly, and went into her bedroom. She sat on the bed, removed her earrings, and dialed the Kerrs' number.

Marian answered it on the first ring. "Hello?" she said.

"Marian? This is Laura Ponti. I'm sorry to be calling so late. I just thought you might like to know I've taken Robert to the train station."

"What?" asked Marian.

"I found Robert on the road and drove him to the station. I thought you might be worried."

"I'm sorry," said Marian. "I don't know what you're talking about. Why did you bring him to the train station?"

"Because that is where he wanted to go."

"Where's John?"

"John?"

"I thought you'd lost your keys. John was returning them."

"No, my keys are intact. Please tell Lyle I called. And thank you so much for the lovely dinner. Good night."

"Good night," said Marian. She hung up the phone, and sat on the bed, trying to figure out what was happening. It was as if they were all playing some game and had left her out. She was sitting there when she heard the car return. She heard John climb the stairs and walk down the hall. He opened the door and saw her.

"What's wrong?" he asked.

"You tell me," she said. "Laura Ponti just called. She said she picked Robert up and took him to the train station."

"She found him?" said John. "Good."

"What's good?" asked Marian. "What's going on?"

"Robert and Lyle had a fight. Robert ran off into the woods. Lyle tried to follow him and collided with a tree."

"Is he all right?"

"He cut his face. And he's upset."

"Where did you go?" asked Marian.

"Looking for Robert. I should tell Lyle Mrs. Ponti found him. I'm sure he's worried."

"He lied to me," said Marian. "He told me Laura had left her keys here. That you had gone to return them."

"I'll be right back," said John. He walked down the hall and knocked on the door of the yellow room.

"Yes?" Lyle said.

John opened the door. "It's me," he said.

Lyle was sitting up in bed. He looked to John like a child, sitting there expectantly, a window of moonlight falling across him. "Did you find him?"

"No," said John. "But Laura Ponti called. She did. She took him to the train station. We thought you'd like to know."

"Yes," said Lyle. "Thanks."

"How's the face?"

"Fine," said Lyle.

"Is there anything I can get you?" asked John.

"No, thanks," said Lyle.

"I told Marian," said John. "Just so you know."

Lyle nodded. "I'm sorry about all this," he said.

"Don't be," said John. "These things happen."

"Is he O.K.?" Marian asked, when John had returned to their bed.

"Yes," said John.

"Poor Lyle," she said. "What did they fight about?"

"I don't know," said John. "Lyle didn't want me to tell you. He wants to tell you in the morning."

"Why did he lie to me? That isn't like him."

"He's ashamed, I think. And—and I don't know. Upset."

After a moment Marian said, "So we were right."

"Oh, Marian," said John.

"What?"

"You sound so mean. It's nothing to be proud of."

Marian didn't answer.

"I want to go to sleep," said John. He rolled over, away from her, and lay still. He heard Marian crying, and felt her shaking beside him. He closed his eyes and listened for a moment, and then he rolled back, toward her, and held her.

Lyle remained sitting up in bed. What do you do, he wondered, when you have failed so miserably to live your life. When you would like to beat your life into the ground with a stick. Smack it until it is nothing but dust.

He got out of bed and stood by the window. The croquet mallets lay like discarded weapons on the lawn. The tablecloth, which had been left out on the table, fluttered in a breeze. But other than that, the world was very still and quiet, except for the continual sound of the river flowing. Lyle turned away from the window. He sat on the edge of his bed and rested his head in his hands.

They smelled strangely of dirt, or blood. He held them in front of his face and breathed through them. He was holding his face on. He wondered if he would ever see Robert again. I'll call him when I get back, he thought, and apologize. Apologize for what? For being honest? For not leading him on? But I led him on a little. Oh, but that is life: you meet someone and lead them on or they lead you on and you move forward. It is not such a bad thing. You would get nowhere if you were never led on.

He went into the bathroom to wash his hands and face. The moon had swung around and was shining in the front of the house now, and Lyle noticed the open door at the far end of the hall, the room there full of moonlight. He walked toward it. He stood in the doorway for a moment, looking in at the two beds standing side by side, the bedspreads pulled tightly across them with Marian's deft hands. He sat down on the bed. There are things you lose you do not get back. You cannot have them, ever again, except in the smudging carbon copy of memory. There are things that seem irreconcilable that you must find a way to reconcile with. The simple passage of days dulls the sharpness of the pain, but it never wears it out: what gets washed away in time gets washed away, and then you are left with a hard cold nub of something, an unlosable souvenir. A little china dachshund from the White Mountains. A shadow puppet from Bali. Look— an ivory shoehorn from a four-star hotel in Zurich. And here, like a stone I carry everywhere, is a bit of someone's heart I have saved from a journey I once made.

22

Lyle was in bed reading Sigrid's book. John and Marian and Tony were downstairs playing cards around the library table. Lyle was tired but he didn't want to go to sleep. He wanted to stay awake until Tony came to bed, for his favorite part of the day was its conclusion: the moments before they fell asleep, talking together in bed. After a while he heard John and Marian come up the stairs and walk to their room at the far end of the hall. He wondered if they would try again to make a baby. He waited for Tony and fell asleep waiting and when he woke up he was still alone. He was not sure how late it was. He went downstairs. All the rooms were dark. He stood in the kitchen, thinking that Tony must have left somehow after all, when he saw him outside, sitting at the table beneath the mulberry tree, smoking. Tony had been a real smoker but now he smoked only occasionally, alone, late at night.

Lyle opened the door and walked across the grass. He sat down across the table from Tony. Tony extinguished his cigarette.

"You can finish it," said Lyle.

"I know," said Tony. "I don't want to."

"Come to bed," said Lyle.

"What time is it?" asked Tony.

"I don't know. Late. I've been waiting for you. I fell asleep."

"It's been such a nice day," said Tony. "A perfect day. I'm glad I stayed."

"So am I," said Lyle.

"I don't want it to end," said Tony.

"Come to bed," said Lyle. "It's time."

They were quiet a moment.

"Did you finish the book?" Tony asked.

"Almost," said Lyle. "It gets quite good. She just works too hard at the beginning, setting it all up."

They sat there in the dark for a moment and then Tony said, "I told Marian."

"What?"

"That I was positive."

"Why?" asked Lyle. "I mean, why now?"

"I don't know. I can't wait forever."

"No," said Lyle. "I suppose not. Did you tell them both? Tonight?"

"No," said Tony. "Just Marian. This afternoon, when we swam to the rock. She'll tell John, I'm sure."

"Yes," said Lyle.

"I'm glad I told her," said Tony. "I feel relieved."

"Good," said Lyle.

"I don't want to get sick," said Tony.

Lyle didn't say anything.

"I think I'm more scared of being sick than I am of dying," said Tony. "Isn't that odd? I'm actually not really scared of dying. I suppose because it's so abstract. I can't imagine it. I'm too literal. But I can imagine being sick. I don't want to be sick."

"Of course you don't," said Lyle. "I don't want you to be sick either."

"I can feel it coming, I think," said Tony.

"What do you feel?" asked Lyle.

"Just scared of being sick in a way that makes me feel that it's near. That it's already happening, somewhere."

"You look fine," said Lyle. "You haven't lost any more weight, have you?"

"No," said Tony. "A little, maybe. I haven't weighed myself lately. I don't really want to know."

"I think you should try not to worry about it. The less you worry, the healthier you'll be."

"That's easy for you to say," said Tony.

"I know," said Lyle. "But it's true."

"I know," said Tony. He paused, and then said, "In a way, I'd like to die now."

"Why?" asked Lyle.

"I guess because I'm a coward. I'd like to die before it gets horrible. I was just thinking if I died now, on a beautiful day like today, my life—I don't know. Do you think it's all relative and when I'm sick it won't be so bad? Not as bad as I think it will be, and I'll be happy to be alive? Happy to be sick and miserable and dying but alive?"

"I don't know," said Lyle. "I think you have to wait and see."

"Maybe it's like a vacation," said Tony.

"What?" asked Lyle.

"Death. No—I mean life. Maybe life is like a vacation. You know how on vacations you always pretend you're having such a good time, but really—especially toward the end—you can't wait to get home? All you want to do is get home and sleep in your own bed. Maybe life is like that. Maybe you realize that at the end, and you just want to get back. Maybe we're just on vacation and we don't know it."

"Maybe," said Lyle.

They sat for a moment.

"Don't cry, Lyle," Tony said. "Don't be sad now. Come and sit over here."

Lyle got up and sat down next to Tony. Tony held him. "I feel better now that we've had this talk," he said. "I know you don't, but I do. Thank you."

After a moment Tony said, "I love you."

Lyle didn't answer.

"Do you know what your problem is?" asked Tony.

"What?" said Lyle.

"That in your life love is the subtext, not the text. It never gets expressed directly. It's suggested, not stated."

"You know I love you," said Lyle.

"Yes," said Tony, "I do. But sometimes I wish I didn't need to try so hard to know it. It shouldn't require effort on my part."

"I'm sorry," said Lyle. "I love you."

"I know," said Tony.

They were silent a moment. "I saw a fox before," Tony said. "Before you came out. It hurried across the lawn. I think foxes are remarkable: they're both feline and canine. I'd like to be a fox." He paused. "Do you want to go for a swim?"

"It's too cold," said Lyle.

"I know," said Tony, "but it will feel good. Come, swim with me, Lyle. And then we'll go to sleep."

"All right," said Lyle.

They stood and walked down to the river and swam, quietly, in the darkness, and then they ran up to the house and got in bed, where gradually, by virtue of holding one another, they grew warm.

23

Only dogs and cats and sleeping drunks and old women hastening toward church inhabited the streets of the East Village when Robert returned. He climbed the six narrow flights up to his apartment. Hector, his friend and roommate, was in the shower. Robert poured himself a glass of juice, and sat at the table. He heard Hector get out of the shower and go into his room. He was singing a song Robert didn't recognize. Hector never sang when Robert was around. He had a terrible voice. After a moment he came in the kitchen. He had on shorts but no shirt.

"Hey," said Hector, "what are you doing back so early?"

"I bolted," said Robert.

"What happened?" Hector sat down.

"I just had to get out of there."

"I told you weekends in the country with heterosexuals could be dangerous to your mental health," said Hector. "Was it awful? Did you eat hamburgers and play croquet?"

"No," said Robert.

"How was Lyle?"

"Weird," said Robert.

"How weird?"

"I don't know. Maybe it was me. All of a sudden, things just kind of fell apart."

"What things?" asked Hector.

"Well, his friends were about the most uptight people I've ever met. I could tell they resented me from the minute I got there. Then I overheard them dumping on me. And when I tried to talk about it with Lyle he freaked out."

"It sounds very unenlightened," said Hector. "Listen, I'm going to Jones Beach with David. Why don't you come? You deserve to have some fun this weekend."

"I'm tired," said Robert. "I didn't sleep at all last night."

"You can sleep on the beach."

"I want to sleep in my bed. Plus I have to work tonight."

"O.K.," said Hector. "Well, maybe we can go out when you get off. I'll stop by."

"O.K.," said Robert.

"I'm sorry you had a shitty weekend," said Hector. "Can I borrow your sunglasses?"

When Hector was gone, Robert lay down on his bed. He was too tired to get undressed. He looked up at the cracked ceiling. He turned over and cocooned his head with his arms, pressing his face into the crook of one elbow. He lay like that for a long time, listening to the noise of the city, before he finally fell asleep.

Nina had always been an indecently late riser, but Laura decided to wait for her before having breakfast. She made a pot of coffee and then set the table out by the pool. She sat in the chair she had sat in the previous morning, waiting again for Nina.

She waited patiently until noon and then she went inside and knocked softly on Nina's door. There was no answer. Laura pushed the door open a bit and stuck her head inside. The bed was empty, neatly made. There was a note on it. She walked over and looked at it for a moment before she picked it up. She irrationally thought it might be an invitation. Nina was inviting her to something. But no. The note read: "I thought it better not to stay. We took a taxi to the train. I hope you had a nice dinner." It wasn't signed, but there was a P.S.: "Anders thanks you for your hospitality." Laura sat on the bed and reread it several times.

She didn't want to be in the house and she didn't want to see the table set by the pool. She didn't know where to go. She would have to get in the car and drive someplace. Get lost again. She went outside, but instead of getting in the car, she walked down the driveway and into the woods. She walked far enough so that she couldn't see the driveway, or the house, or the road. Just woods all around her, summer woods, dense and buttered with sunlight.

Lyle woke up with a black eye. He had never had a black eye before. He stood for a while, looking at it in the bathroom mirror. It was such an ugly thing: the purple and yellow stain of it on his face. He wanted to stay away from everyone until it disappeared, but he knew that was impossible, so he went down to breakfast.

Roland was ensconced in his high chair at the table.

Marian was sitting next to him, feeding him some yogurt. "Oh, my God," she said, as Lyle entered the room. "Your eye!"

"Yes," said Lyle. He sat down.

"Does it hurt?" asked Marian.

"No," said Lyle. "I'd rather not talk about it."

"Of course," said Marian. "Here, let me get you some coffee."

"I'll get it," said Lyle. He stood up and poured himself a cup of coffee. "Where's John?" he asked.

"Where do you think?" said Marian. She nodded toward the garden.

Lyle sat at the table for a moment, drinking his coffee, watching Marian feed Roland. "Could I do that?" he asked. "Could I feed him?"

"Of course," said Marian. "Do you want Uncle Lyle to feed you?" she asked Roland.

Roland seemed not to care.

"Here," Marian said, handing the spoon to Lyle. "He's hungry. Just give him little spoonfuls till he won't take anymore. He'll turn his head away when he's had enough."

Lyle held the first spoonful out to Roland, who eyed it, and Lyle, for a moment, and then somewhat reluctantly opened his mouth. Lyle gently inserted the spoon. "Good boy," he said.

Marian watched them and said, "It's a lovely day. A little cooler than yesterday."

"Good," said Lyle.

"We have nothing planned. Just a lazy day."

"Good," said Lyle.

They sat in silence, intent on the feeding of Roland. Finally he turned his head away. "Finished?" asked Lyle. "No more?"

"You did very well," said Marian. "Let me wipe his face off." She got up and dampened a cloth.

"Let me," said Lyle. He wiped the yogurt from around Roland's small mouth. Then he picked him up, out of the high chair, and held him against his chest. "Can I ask you a question?" he said to Marian.

"Of course you may," said Marian.

"Did you like Robert?"

Marian thought for a moment. "No," she said. "I don't think I did. But it's hard to know, because, well, I didn't really get to know him, did I? It was all so strained yesterday, and then with his running off like that. Why do you ask? Lyle, tell me. What happened last night?"

"Robert had the feeling you didn't like him," said Lyle.

"Did he? That's a shame."

"Actually, he said he overheard you telling John you didn't like him."

Marian didn't say anything for a moment, and then she said, "Why did you do that?"

"What?" asked Lyle.

"Ask me that question, when you knew the answer. Why did you try to trap me like that?"

"I didn't mean to trap you," said Lyle.

"You didn't?" asked Marian. "Then what did you mean?"

"I don't know," said Lyle. "I wanted to know what you'd tell me. What you'd say to me."

"You didn't think I'd tell you the truth?" asked Marian.

"I don't know," said Lyle. "I'm confused. Yesterday you told me you liked him."

"Well, I did, yesterday. At least I was trying hard to. And I still would be, today, if he were here. Besides, I don't make decisions about whether I like people or not on the basis of a few hours in their company."

"I think Robert thought you had."

"I'm sorry he thought that. Is that why he left? Because he thought I didn't like him?"

"He didn't think it. He knew it. Or thought he knew it. He heard you say it."

"Well, I'm sorry," said Marian. "I was trying to be nice to him. I was trying to like him. I'm sorry if he overheard me say something that hurt him."

"You don't have to be sorry," said Lyle.

"Oh?" said Marian. "Don't I? Isn't that what you're saying? That this is all my fault?"

"No," said Lyle. "Not at all. It's my fault, if anyone's. He didn't leave because you didn't like him. He left because he thought *I* didn't like him. Or love him. He wanted me to tell him I loved him, and I wouldn't. So he panicked, and ran away."

"He sounds like a spoiled baby," said Marian.

"He is," said Lyle. "We all are, deep down. Some of us are just better at hiding it than others."

"I disagree," said Marian. "I don't think it's a matter of hiding anything. I think it's a matter of learning how to behave responsibly and respectfully. Learning how to consider other people. You don't run off into the night just because someone won't tell you that they love you. That's hardly the behavior of a rational adult."

"Yes," said Lyle. "I know it isn't."

"You need to find somebody, Lyle—in time, at the right time—some adult, somebody who understands who you are. Robert may have been very sweet, but I don't think he was that person. Do you?"

"No," said Lyle. "But—"

"But what?"

"I liked him. Nevertheless, I liked him very much."

"Well, of course you liked him. I understand that: he wasn't stupid, was he, and he was good-looking, and he adored you. It's no wonder you liked him. But that doesn't mean he was right for you, does it?"

"No," said Lyle. "In fact, that's what I told him, last night."

"You told him that?"

"Yes. He asked me."

"Well, I suppose he deserved it then, if he asked you. In that case, I think you should just forget about him and have a pleasant day. The weekend's only half over, you know. You're not leaving until this evening, are you?"

"Yes," said Lyle. "Or late this afternoon."

"Good," said Marian. "I thought maybe we could take a picnic lunch up the river in the punt. How does that sound?"

"That sounds fine," said Lyle. There was a pause, and then Lyle said, "What punt?"

"I meant the rowboat," said Marian.

"Then why did you call it a punt?"

"I don't know," said Marian. "I suppose because I like

the idea of a punt. I like to think of it as a punt. Is that a crime?"

"No," said Lyle. "Of course not."

"Then why did you correct me? Do you think I romanticize everything?"

"A little," said Lyle. "Sometimes."

"Oh," said Marian. "Well, I suppose you're right. But I don't see the harm in it. Really, I don't. It doesn't hurt anyone, does it? To call a rowboat a punt?"

"No," said Lyle, "of course it doesn't. It's just that between us, between you and me, I . . . I see no need. I want things to be honest between us, and clear."

"I thought they were," said Marian. "Have I been deluding myself about that as well?"

They were silent a moment. "Is he sleeping?" Marian asked. She meant Roland.

"No," said Lyle. He looked down at Roland. "He's wide awake. Alert as can be. He seems very alert for his age."

"Does he?" said Marian. "Do you really think so?"

"Well, as far as I can tell. I don't know many babies. But look at him watching me. He's definitely thinking something."

"I think it's your eye," said Marian. "It's quite colorful. Does it hurt?"

"No," said Lyle. "A little. Yes."

"Aren't you supposed to put steak on it? I think I've got some I could defrost."

"Don't bother," said Lyle. "It's fine."

Marian reached out her arms. Lyle handed the baby to her. She held him and looked down at him. "Sometimes I'm scared," she said.

"Of what?"

"Of Roland. Of how much I love him. He keeps me sane, and alive. And I think he shouldn't. That it's not right. That it's I who should do that for him."

"Well, can't it work both ways?" asked Lyle.

Marian didn't answer. She was crying. Lyle watched her. He did not know what to say.

Nina answered on the first ring with a breathless, terse hello.

"Nina," said Laura, "it's your mother."

"Oh," said Nina. "Hello."

"I'm calling to tell you I'm sorry about last night. I'm sorry about how I behaved and I'm sorry you left. I'm very sorry you left. I hope it doesn't mean you won't come up again."

"I don't know," said Nina. "The schedule's been changed. We're going up to Toronto next week."

"Toronto? What for?"

"They were having trouble getting permits in New York or something. I'm not sure. There was just a message on my machine when I got back."

"When do you head up there?"

"I'm not sure. Thursday, I think."

"And what are you doing till then?"

"What do you mean?"

"I mean are you occupied in the meantime? Perhaps you could spend the early part of the week up here. With Anders, of course."

"Listen," said Nina, "could I call you back? You caught me at a bad time. I was just headed out."

"Of course," said Laura. "You have the number. Call whenever you're free. I'll be here."

"I think I left my sunglasses up there," said Nina. "Did you find them?"

"I don't think I've seen them," said Laura. "I'll look, though. Would they be in your room?"

"Yes," said Nina. "Or by the pool. I think I might have left them outside. Or in the bathroom, maybe. I'm not sure. Maybe I left them on the train."

"Well, I'll look," said Laura.

"I've got to go," said Nina.

"All right," said Laura. "Will you call me later?"

"Yes," said Nina.

"I hope you can come," said Laura.

"Yes," said Nina. "I'll see. I'll call you back. I'll probably be out late, so it might not be till tomorrow."

"That would be fine," said Laura.

"All right, I'll talk to you later. Bye." Nina hung up.

Laura stood for a moment in the kitchen, looking out at the table by the pool, which was still set for breakfast. The napkins had blown off into the bushes. Well, she thought, that's that. It's all up to Nina now.

By late Sunday afternoon, when Marian drove Lyle to the station, the light had gone stark and was illuminating the trees with a force and clarity that suggested autumn. Yet it was still midsummer.

Marian parked and Lyle opened the door, but Marian touched his arm and said, "No, we're early. Stay a minute."

Lyle pulled the door closed. Marian dusted the steering wheel with her middle finger, round and round, and then looked at it: clean. "I feel so . . . awful," she said. "About what's happened, this weekend."

"Why?" asked Lyle.

"I feel it was my fault," said Marian. "What happened with Robert."

"I told you," said Lyle. "It wasn't your fault."

"Actually," said Marian, "that's not what I think you told me. Or at least it's not what I felt you told me."

"It was something between us," said Lyle. "It had nothing to do with you."

"No, I've been thinking about it. When you arrived yesterday you were both so happy."

"Yes," said Lyle. "We were. But it wasn't you."

"I wasn't nice to him," said Marian.

Lyle said nothing. He looked down the empty curve of track, but there was no train.

"But you see it wasn't about him, how I was behaving," said Marian.

"What was it about?" asked Lyle.

Marian looked at him as if he were simple. "It was about Tony," she said. "It was about you and Tony."

"Oh," said Lyle.

"I couldn't allow myself to be nice to him, I was awful to him, I drove him away—I know I did—because of Tony."

"I think the train is coming," said Lyle.

"You like him, don't you?" Marian asked.

"Yes," said Lyle. "I like—liked—him very much. But for reasons that have become obvious we are—we are not well suited."

"Will you invite him back?"

"No," said Lyle. "Besides, he'd never come." He opened the door and stepped out of the car.

"But ask him," said Marian. "Promise me you will. Or should I call him? Why don't you give me his number and I'll call him? I'll talk to him. I'll try to explain myself."

"Let me talk to him first," said Lyle.

"Call me," said Marian. "As soon as you have."

"I will." He closed the door.

"Wait," said Marian.

Lyle leaned into the open window. "What?" he asked.

"Are we still friends, Lyle?"

"Of course we're friends," said Lyle.

"You wouldn't lie to me, would you? About something as important as that?"

"No," said Lyle. "Look—here's the train. I'll call you." He hurried up the stairs to the platform. There was an overpass above the tracks, and Marian watched him run across it and descend the stairs on the opposite side, where she lost sight of him behind the arriving, and then departing, train.

When she returned from the train station the house seemed very still and empty. It was empty. John and Roland were in the garden. She went upstairs and stripped the bed Lyle had used. She found a small watercolor of an Adirondack chair on the floor. She picked it up and studied it. The chair was alone, floating, a little puddle of deep green shadow beneath it. It was like a chair in heaven. It was beautiful. Of course Robert had done it. It was beautiful and Robert had made it. She put the painting on the bedside table and looked out the window. The shadows were long and dark. They looked spilled across the lawn, eloquent. She took the sheets down to the laundry room. There was nothing to do for dinner. They were going to go out for dinner. She walked about the house for a while, as if she were looking for something, or inspecting for damage. But everything was fine. Then she went out the back door and down the lawn, to the garden.

"Did Lyle get off all right?" John asked.

"Yes," she said.

"Are you getting hungry?"

"Yes," she said.

"Would you hold up these tomatoes while I stake them?"

"Yes." Marian opened the gate and entered the garden. Roland sat in the dirt, playing with a few cherry tomatoes and a blue-jay feather.

"He's fine," said John. "I've kept my eye on him." He

indicated the plant to be staked. Marian held it up while John cut a length of twine from a ball and began to secure it.

"John," Marian said.

"What?" asked John.

"Do you think I'm a good person?"

He looked up at her. "Of course, I do," he said. "You are. Why do you ask that?"

"Because," she said. "Suddenly, I don't feel sure."

"Do you mean because of this weekend?"

"Yes," said Marian. "Although not only. I just feel, suddenly, not like a good person. I feel"—she paused—"bad."

"This weekend was difficult," said John. "For everyone. But that's ridiculous. You're a fine person. You mustn't feel like that."

"But I do," said Marian. "Here." She removed her hand from the plant and touched her breast. The plant collapsed beneath its burdens of fruit. "Inside. I feel mean and selfish. And foolish. Unkind."

John sat back on his haunches. "What did Lyle say to you?"

"Nothing," said Marian. "This isn't about Lyle. It's about me."

"No—" John began.

"Yes," Marian said. "To some extent, I know it's true. I know it. I can feel it so clearly. I don't"—and she shook her head, vehemently—"I don't like myself." She began to cry.

So did Roland. He sat on the ground with the tomatoes in his hands and wailed. Marian picked him up. "Oh, I'm sorry, my sweetness," she said. "Did I upset you? I'm sorry, I'm sorry," she said, patting his tiny back.

John watched this all, a little stunned. When Roland stopped crying, he said, "Here. Give him to me."

Marian handed Roland to John. They stood there for a moment.

"I know if you feel bad I can't tell you not to feel bad," said John. "But—it's perfectly natural. Your relationship with Lyle is complicated. I know you love him very much. He knows that, too, I'm sure. And sometimes that's difficult. Love makes things difficult sometimes. You know that."

"I don't know," said Marian. "Suddenly I don't know what I know. I feel very unsure of what I know."

"Everyone feels that way sometimes," said John. "I don't think that's such a bad thing."

"Maybe not," said Marian. "But it's frightening."

Roland began to squirm in John's arms. "Should we go eat?" John asked.

"Yes," said Marian.

"What do you feel like?"

"I don't know."

"Why don't we stay here? I'll make dinner," said John.

"What will you make?" asked Marian.

"What about pancakes? Do you want pancakes?"

"That would be fine," said Marian.

"Do we have syrup?"

"Of course," said Marian.

"I haven't made pancakes in ages," said John. "I hope I remember all my secrets."

They walked up the lawn toward the house. It stood there solid and empty, waiting, ready to hold them.

Lyle fell asleep on the train. He awoke just as it was slipping beneath the Tappan Zee Bridge. A woman across the aisle from him nodded and smiled. She looked vaguely familiar, so he smiled back.

"What happened to your eye?" she asked.

Lyle touched the tender flesh along his cheekbone. "I walked into a tree," he said. "It was very stupid."

He turned away and looked out the window at the river flowing beside them. It looked a little blurred, like a painting of itself. The water was choppy, blown by the wind into quick translucent crests. The sun was low in the sky and refracted in the window. He could see his own reflection, and through that, flickering in the glass, the reflection of what was ahead. Lyle thought, coming back to the city is always nicer, in a way, because you travel in the same direction as the river.

As they entered the tunnel the woman across from him stood up and pulled a bag down from the rack. She was the delft woman, Lyle realized. It had only been yesterday he sat next to her, yet it seemed ages ago. He stood, and walked behind her down the aisle.

As they waited in the vestibule for the doors to open, she turned around and looked at him. "Did you have a nice weekend?" she asked.

What could he say? He could not say no. "Yes," he said. "How about you?"